# Dark Angel

## Felicity Heaton

# HER ANGEL: BOUND WARRIORS SERIES

Dark Angel
Fallen Angel
Warrior Angel
Bound Angel

Find out more at: www.felicityheaton.com

# CHAPTER 1

The images in the bright pool flickered past Apollyon's eyes at lightning speed but he could see them all, could bring each into focus and pause there a moment to understand what was happening in the scene before discarding it and allowing the flow to resume. It was a distraction he used daily, his every hour devoted to watching over the mortals.

In the long centuries he had studied the human world, he had seen a million or more changes, from the smallest accidental discovery to the grandest scheme that had altered the future of the race.

He had witnessed the growth of the mortals.

He had watched them forget his kind.

No one believed in angels anymore.

And his master had not called him forth from the bottomless pit in Hell in all the time he had been assigned to the dark realm of smoke and fire, hundreds of years passed choking on the stench of sulphur and bearing the presence of demons, and the king of Hell's vicious taunts that rang in his ears on a daily basis.

Yet Apollyon waited for the call to come, faithful and patient, committed to his duty even as others around him chose to live by their own commands. He had heard the tales from angels who had reason to enter Hell, whispers and rumours about how their fellow warriors had softened and fallen for mortal women, their devotion wavering and their commitment altering to their love.

He would do no such thing.

He had no interest in mortals.

His dark blue gaze darted around the silvery pool, following the history it was recording, stopping a moment on images that interested him.

Wars. Death. Bloodshed.

It was something that never changed. The one constant. Mortals seemed bent on destroying each other.

One day, his master would call him and Earth would know the true meaning of destruction.

The pool cast pale light on him and the jagged obsidian rocks that surrounded it, chasing back the bleak darkness of Hell.

He rolled his shoulders as he crouched near it with his elbows resting on his bare knees, his hands dangling in front of him. The intricate gold metalwork on the black greaves protecting his shins and the vambraces around his forearms caught the light and shone, reminding him of how it would reflect the sunlight when he flew.

A dull ache started behind his breastbone.

On a weary sigh, Apollyon stood and unfurled his black wings, unable to deny the need to feel air in his feathers.

The chest plate of his armour rode up his torso as he lifted his arms and stretched them too. He tilted his head back, another long sigh escaping him as he stared at the endless black ceiling of the cavern above him, a barrier that separated him from the sky he longed to fly in once again.

A sky he hadn't seen in too long.

If it hadn't been for the pool, he would have forgotten the blue of it, and the green of the grass and the trees, the bright colours of flowers. He would have forgotten the clear air and crystalline waters. He would no longer remember the breathtaking mountains and wide stretching plains.

He would only know the glowing gold of the fires that dotted the black cragged landscape that surrounded him, and the rivers of lava that snaked between onyx mountains and around the plateau he stood upon. He would only know the choking stench of the smoke that laced the air.

He would only know the darkness that swirled around him, as thick as oil in the air, a constant presence that he couldn't shake—could only bear.

Apollyon closed his eyes, shutting out Hell as he built a picture in his mind, formed an image that stirred a memory.

One where he had been flying, breathing fresh air and feeling it beat against him as the sun warmed his wings.

He heaved another sigh as the ache in his chest worsened, birthing a desire to soar above the cities again, unseen and unknown, and to speak with the angels who walked on Earth and watched over the mortals.

He longed to be free of the choking fires of Hell.

He forced himself to open his eyes and see the home that was his now, a place he couldn't escape without an order from his master.

A realm he despised.

He went to turn away from the torture of watching the world he couldn't experience and paused as his blue gaze caught on an image as it rippled across the silvery liquid.

He frowned and crouched again, the long strands of his black hair falling forwards to brush the skin exposed between the slats of his hip armour and his knees as he leaned forwards and stared at the image he had stopped before him.

A lone female.

It wasn't the first time he had seen her. Noticed her. The petite blonde liked to walk in the park alone these days and her expression was often troubled, as though she bore a heavy weight on her heart.

What was she thinking when she looked like that?

It was the first time he had wondered about a mortal, had found questions filling his mind as he watched and studied them rather than simply absorbing facts about the things he was seeing.

If he was feeling honest with himself, he would admit that the park wasn't the only place he had spotted her.

He had seen her indirectly too, picking her out of a crowd or glimpsing her passing through an image that had interested him, and each time his gaze had followed her until she had disappeared from view.

Now, she stood staring up at the Eiffel Tower and the clear blue sky beyond it, her back to him and the gentle breeze catching her short red dress and tousling her long fair hair. He didn't need to see her face to know that it was her.

No other mortal captivated him as she could.

Roses framed the view, obscuring much of her legs.

He cocked his head and ran his gaze over what he could see. He had never seen her dressed like this. She had always worn layers of clothing in the past, her legs covered and a thick black coat encasing her slender frame.

The seasons had passed so quickly and he hadn't noticed that it was summer where she was in Europe.

The image changed, panning up the height of the Eiffel Tower, and he wanted it to go back to her until he saw the stretching blue sky above the top of the tower.

Apollyon reached out to the pool, desperate to touch that sky and feel the sun beating down on his wings as he flew.

The image drifted away, replaced with a succession of others that he had no interest in as one thought spun through his mind.

It was summer.

He stood and imagined flying in that blue sky and how exhilarating it would be. He pictured the whole of Paris stretched out below him, the elegant stone buildings bright in the sunlight that would warm their dull grey roofs and the tree-lined avenues filled with mortals coming and going, enjoying the weather.

He had never been there but he knew it well from the images he had seen, had witnessed it grow from small simple buildings into a grand bustling city.

What would it be like to see such a place?

To see such a female in the flesh?

He shook that thought away. He had no interest in mortal women.

If he didn't, why did his heart stop whenever he saw her?

Apollyon looked back into the pool and then turned away from it. His duty was to his master. He had to remain here, guardian of the bottomless pit, suffering the acrid fires of Hell, until his master called him.

He chuckled mirthlessly at that.

No one was going to call him. He was going to spend the rest of eternity trapped in his own personal Hell.

A dark curse rolled off his tongue and a noise like thunder rumbled in the distance. A taunting voice echoed within it, attempting to fill his mind with poison. He shut the Devil out, refusing to succumb to the temptations he offered to all angels who entered his domain. He wasn't weak, an angel easy to sway. He was strong, easily pushed back against the Devil because he had been made to fight him.

As the wretch's voice faded, a sense that someone was speaking his name built inside him. He listened, trying to hear the voice of his master, sure that this time it wasn't the Devil provoking him because the feeling it evoked in him was different.

Familiar.

But no matter what he did, no matter how fiercely he strained, he couldn't discern where the call was coming from.

He could only feel it beating inside him, growing stronger by the second.

Tugging him upwards.

Apollyon grabbed his sword, buckled the sheath to his waist, and didn't wait for the call to come again. This was his chance to escape Hell and he would take it. He was finally being called. He had a mission again at last.

He spread his black wings and with a single strong beat lifted into the thick air. The wind from them blew the dark smoke back so it swirled beneath him as they raised him higher and higher, carrying him towards the ceiling of his prison.

He stretched a hand up to it.

The black rock parted before him.

He beat his wings harder, flying faster now as a streak of blue formed above him. Hundreds of feet of rock passed him in a blur and he could hardly breathe, struggled to contain the feelings colliding inside him as he exploded into the fresh air on the other side. He grinned and shot upwards, his black wings beating furiously against the warm air, and didn't stop until he reached the clouds.

Apollyon hovered there, casting his dark blue eyes over the world at his feet, the cooler air streaming through his long black hair.

It was as beautiful as he remembered, more so in fact.

The cities the mortals had built fascinated him, had him itching to see them with his own eyes at last, to experience what his fellow warriors could and see if everything lived up to the tales they had told him and the reports he had read.

But his mission came first.

Perhaps if he fulfilled it in a satisfactory manner, he would be allowed some freedom, could soak in the mortal world before he returned to his duties.

He swooped lower, searching for his mission and listening for his master's call.

What did he desire him to do?

Whatever it was, he would carry it out. He always did. He had destroyed many cities in his name and cast many sinners into the bottomless pit. He had fought the Devil and defeated him, keeping him contained in Hell. Whatever challenge his master presented, he would complete it.

He frowned when he saw the city stretched below him.

Paris.

The desire to go to the Eiffel Tower and find the mortal female was strong but he resisted it and flew over the city, seeking the source of the call and his mission.

The call was quieter now though, weaker than it had been in Hell, and he struggled to locate the source of it as he flew along streets and above avenues, invisible to mortal eyes.

It burned within him though, relentless and driving him to search, even when he was beginning to wonder if he would be searching forever and if this was just a cruel joke because he had cursed.

The Devil would do such a despicable thing. He had a strong voice and could throw it well, could have easily feigned retreat, making Apollyon think he had shut him out, only to trick him into thinking the other voice he had heard was a different one—that of his master.

The bastard had promised Apollyon that he would pay for all the times he had cast him back into Hell after all.

Was it possible this was a lie? A trick? Was it possible he had been so desperate to leave Hell that he had fallen foul of the Devil?

Apollyon swooped lower, effortlessly cutting through the warmer air, using the feel of it tickling his black feathers and washing over his skin to distract him from his troubling thoughts. Fears that were unfounded.

It wasn't the Devil who had lured him to Paris.

It wasn't.

Turning, he dived down a side street, skimming low above the heads of the mortals, causing a wind to gust against them. He smiled when they shrieked and grabbed their clothes to keep them in place. It was wrong to take such childish pleasure from doing such things, but all angels had a tendency to misuse their invisibility and he was sure it wouldn't be held against him by his superiors.

A strong beat of his wings and he was soaring upwards again, determined to find the source of the call that tugged at his chest.

He landed on the edge of the roof of an old pale stone building and looked across the city towards the Eiffel Tower. It speared the clear sky, surrounded by lush green at the base, a beacon that called to him as fiercely as the voice.

He pushed off in that direction and froze.

Someone was speaking his name again.

Apollyon focused, frowning as he scanned the city and tried to discern the direction it was coming from. His gaze shot back to the Eiffel Tower. There?

He ran to the far edge of the building and leaped off, waiting until he was close to the flagstones of the square below before he unfurled his wings and beat them, shooting straight across the square only a few feet above the ground. He ducked and weaved through the people and came out over a grassy bank. The river was ahead and beyond it the Eiffel Tower. He flew straight for it and then came to an abrupt halt in mid-air when he heard the call again.

It was behind him.

He scoured the people below. Was his master down there, amongst them, calling to him?

His master had several guises. Apollyon's eyes darted over the mortals, stopping for barely a second on each face. None of them matched how he remembered his master.

The call came more clearly this time, beating deep in his heart.

His gaze shot in the direction it had come from.

His eyes widened.

*Her?*

A fair-haired mortal female stood beside one of the fountains below, her back to him and the warm breeze playing with the short skirt of her dark red dress. The jets of water from the fountains sprayed high, the droplets catching the wind to reveal a rainbow and settling on his skin when it blew towards him.

Apollyon frowned.

It had to be the Devil's work.

He had been watching her, had cursed, and then she had called him.

It was ridiculous.

No mortal had the power to call an angel, and he had not had a different master since eternity began, although he didn't remember those days, had forgotten it all the first time he had been reborn and had only the recorded history in Heaven to go on.

Cautiously, Apollyon swooped down, closer to her, hovering barely twenty metres above her head.

Had she called him?

He needed to know, and he would find out.

He was going to speak to her for the first time.

# CHAPTER 2

Apollyon hovered in the air close to the slender petite female, studying her where she stood near the fountains, so focused on her he didn't notice the other mortals coming and going in the busy city around her, didn't hear the blast of the car horns in the distance behind him, or the steady noise of the fountains. He didn't even notice the warmth of the sun on his wings.

All he knew was her.

Had she called him? It seemed so impossible.

She raised a hand to her face and it lingered there. What was she doing? Her shoulders heaved and a wave of sorrow and anger washed over him, giving him pause and pulling him towards her at the same time.

She was hurting.

He turned and flew back along the bridge over the river behind her to land midway along it on the stone balustrade. He stepped down off the low wall and focused on himself. His wings didn't want to disappear and it took several strides towards her before he was sure the mortals wouldn't see them and that the glamour he was casting was falling into place. He altered his clothes, replacing his armour with a fine black suit, with a black shirt and a dark blue tie, and then swept his long hair back and tied it at the nape of his neck with a blue thong.

Finally, he lifted the force that made him invisible to mortal eyes and walked casually towards her. He took the blue handkerchief from his breast pocket, stepped up behind her, and hesitated for only a moment before touching her shoulder.

"Are you alright?" he said in French, hoping he had the right language and the right words.

He hadn't spoken to a mortal in a long time and although he knew modern languages, he had never used them.

She touched her face again, her long fair hair a curtain which he couldn't see beyond, and sniffed.

When she turned to face him, she was smiling.

Her hazel eyes landed on the offered handkerchief at first and then slowly ran up his arm to his chest and then towards his face, heat following in their wake as his breathing slowed to a halt.

She was beautiful.

More so in the flesh than she had appeared in the pool, her features soft and her eyes round, her lips a delicate shade of pink against her clear skin. He stared down at her, captivated, a little lost. She could be an angel herself.

The moment her gaze met his, her expression changed. Her hand stopped close to taking the handkerchief and horror filled her eyes.

"Get away from me." Her French held a sharp note of panic as she shoved past him and stormed towards the bridge.

Apollyon frowned, looked at the handkerchief, and then went after her.

She glanced over her shoulder and her pace increased as she spotted him following her. Despite her best and somewhat confusing efforts, it was easy to close the gap between them. His strides were longer than hers and her little heeled sandals were clearly not made for a swift escape.

"Leave me alone."

Why was she running?

People stared as she pushed through them and as he passed them, murmuring to each other, speculating in different languages about what was happening. He wasn't sure either. She was causing a scene and he wanted to know why. Needed to know.

"Get away from me!" She turned to face him as she reached the middle of the bridge and backed away, the fear still bright in her hazel eyes, flowing around him and filling him with a strange need, a desire to comfort her and ease her. Her eyes darkened as she frowned and spoke as though uttering a curse. "*Abaddon*."

He hadn't heard that name in a long time.

It caught him off guard, had him stopping dead and staring at her as it rang in his mind and the reason for her fear hit him hard.

She knew he was an angel.

How? Had his glamour failed?

It had been millennia since he'd had to cast one, so it was possible.

He looked around at the watching mortals. None of them appeared afraid. If they could see an angel before them as she could, they would be reacting the same as she was, surely? People would be screaming that the

Apocalypse was nigh and the world was going to end, and he would be in serious trouble with his master.

A master who hadn't called him.

She had.

Could she see through the glamour? Was she different somehow to other mortals?

"I don't want to die," she muttered almost beneath her breath and cast a fearful look his way. "Please don't kill me."

Kill her?

Apollyon barely stopped himself from taking a step towards her, the need to comfort her and correct her, to reassure her that he wasn't going to hurt her, rushing through him with the force of a tidal wave.

He clenched his fists beside his hips instead of reaching for her and struggled to make sense of things, to find the way to calm her.

This wasn't going as he had expected. She wasn't supposed to have been able to see that he was an angel. She was supposed to have accepted his kind offer of a handkerchief to dry her tears and told him why she was crying so he could figure out what he was doing here and whether someone was playing a trick on him.

Those tears spilled down her cheeks as she wrapped her arms around herself, making herself small and making him ache to reach out to her again and somehow ease her suffering.

Whatever pain had caused her to cry, it was still strong within her heart, tormenting her. The tears she spilled weren't born of fear of him. They were born of pain. He could *feel* it. There was some sort of link between them, a connection that gave him insight into her feelings and a sense that she needed him and that they were supposed to have met here today.

Which was ridiculous.

A mortal could never call him. They didn't have the voice.

He had been alone too long and was dreaming all of this, seeing things as he wanted them and not with clear eyes.

There was only one way of finding out whether she had called him somehow. He had hoped to discover it through casual conversation but that wasn't an option now. It was time for a more direct approach.

He stepped towards her and she backed away again, holding both of her hands out as though that gesture alone could stop him if he wanted to get to her.

"Please," she whispered and shook her head, sending more tears tumbling down her ashen cheeks.

"Leave her alone." A burly man started towards him.

Apollyon lost patience and cast his hand out, waving it across the gathered crowd. "There is nothing interesting to see here."

Their expressions went slack and they moved as one, drifting off and back into their own lives, moving past him and the mortal woman as though they weren't even there.

Her hazel eyes darted over the other mortals, desperation mounting in them together with a flicker of terror. "Oh God, you're going to kill me."

He frowned at her. "Why would you say such a thing?"

"It's what you do." There was accusation in her tone and a hint of bravery as she visibly steeled herself.

Courage in the face of death?

A moment ago, she had been fleeing him and now she looked ready to fight. Curious little female.

"I have not done such a thing in a very long time." He held back a sigh. It was never going to leave him. Spend a few centuries as the angel of death and no one forgets. Everyone presumes you're still in charge of taking life's final breath from mortals. Still, it was better than the other rumour that he was the Devil. "There is a fleet of angels who do it now."

She didn't look as though she believed him. Her hands trembled in front of her and she swallowed hard.

"I didn't ask for my powers. Please don't take me there." She shook her head, her hazel eyes darting over him as her pale eyebrows furrowed.

"Where?" His patience started to wear thin again as he fought to get his own question out into the open so he could clear a few things up.

She kept distracting him, pushing more questions into his mind that he voiced instead despite his desire to know whether she had called him.

He tracked back over what she had said.

Powers?

"All the fires of Hell are in your wake... I don't want to go there. I haven't done anything wrong." Her light voice trembled slightly as she glanced beyond him.

Apollyon looked behind him. All he could see was Paris. The edge of the stone bridge and the murky river, the fountain and square, and the city beyond.

"You are gifted." He looked back at her as it hit him, deep into her hazel eyes.

She nodded.

Was this how she had called him?

He frowned and looked at the fountain at the other end of the bridge behind him and then at her. "What were you doing there?"

She looked past him, blinked a few times, and then her eyebrows rose. "Nothing really. Contemplating life, I guess, and how shitty it is."

He was familiar enough with mortal curse words to know she thought her life was bad. Why?

"You did not ask for anything?" He stepped closer to her and this time she didn't back away.

It was a start.

She kept staring at the fountain with wide eyes. Tears lined her lashes. All of her fear disappeared and the pain returned, fiercer than before. She clutched her hands to her chest against her red dress, and he felt the hurt well up inside her, overwhelming her and flowing into him.

"Revenge," she whispered and her gaze darted to him. "I asked for vengeance against that cheating bastard."

Cheating? A sinner?

She had called for vengeance and he had heard her, and he had felt compelled to answer and accept her mission. He couldn't. Contracting with her would break the one between him and his master.

Apollyon looked at her, studying her pale beauty.

She had called him and he had come. She was his master now. He had accepted the mission and the contract the moment he had left Hell.

He was going to get into trouble for this.

It had been a while since he had been on Earth though, and although the angels who watched over mortals now tolerated the old sins and only took them into account at death rather than punished the sinner during their life, he did still hate some of them.

Infidelity in particular.

"Are you really here to kill me?" A hint of colour touched her cheeks when he smiled at her, stirring a strange heat in his veins.

He shook his head. "You called me and I came to you, not to take your life but to ease your suffering."

She swallowed and looked as though she was going to deny that she was in pain.

Apollyon stepped up to her and touched her face, tensed when electricity leaped along his nerves in response to the feel of her warm, soft skin beneath his fingertips. His breath stuttered as he lingered, absorbing how good it felt to touch her. When she began to look nervous again, he forced himself to do as he had meant to before the feel of her had affected him.

He caressed her cheek, placed his fingers under her chin, and raised her eyes to his.

"Whatever he did to you, I will make him suffer for it, but no man is worth such tears," he bit out the words, his dark eyebrows drawing down as anger poured through his veins to obliterate the warmth she had caused in them. "Your heart will heal in time and you will love again."

Her hazel eyes searched his.

Apollyon stared deep into them and that strange warmth returned, travelling along his hand from where his fingertips touched her face. It chased through him, lighting him up inside, and finally settled in his chest, burning there, rousing feelings long forgotten.

Feelings that felt forbidden and dangerous.

"I will give you the revenge you seek."

Those words were distant to his ears even though they issued from his lips.

He was lost in her eyes, in the way they sparkled as she looked at him with so much warmth.

Was it gratitude that made her look that way?

Or was it something else?

"Are you a goddess?" he whispered, trying to keep his thoughts on track and on his mission.

She shook her head, moving his fingers with her, and licked her lips. He made the mistake of looking at them, found himself enraptured as the soft pink tip of her tongue swept over them.

A surge of hunger rushed through him and he snatched his hand away, shocked by the strength of his desire and the suddenness of it.

"I'm a witch," she said, matter of fact, with a little shrug that was stiff and awkward as colour rose onto her cheeks again.

Apollyon stared at her.

Was he making a terrible mistake by helping her? A part of him said to leave now before it was too late and he became too deeply involved with her.

But he couldn't bring himself to do it.

She had cast a spell on him.

And he was a slave to her.

# CHAPTER 3

Serenity's eyes widened and she stepped back when the mountain of a man standing before her drew the sword that hung at his waist. He had changed his mind and was going to kill her after all. She told herself to run, but her body locked up, refusing to cooperate, so she could only stare at him and await her demise.

She wasn't sure what to think when he eased himself down onto one knee in front of her, lowered his head, and held his sword out to her, the hilt and tip of the beautiful blade resting on his upturned palms.

"I am yours to command." His French was perfect, making his deep voice so sexy that a shiver tripped over her skin whenever he spoke.

Was she supposed to do something?

People were staring again as they passed. What did they see? They certainly weren't seeing a man offering a sword to her, that was for sure. To them, did he look as though he was kneeling with his hands raised in supplication?

Was he dressed in black and gold armour that didn't leave much to the imagination?

Did he have huge black feathered wings?

She imagined that he didn't. If he did, the people would probably be screaming rather than merely glancing at him as though he had gone insane.

"Erm, okay." Serenity hesitated before touching the sword. The gleaming steel was cold beneath her fingers. She snatched her hand back, not liking the feel of it, and muttered, "Thanks."

He stood with grace, his muscles shifting beneath his golden skin, and she tried not to stare at his physique. Either he worked out a lot, or angels were naturally endowed with the body of a god.

He was pure perfection as he stood close to her, his broad chest rising and falling, moving the beautifully decorated black breastplate. His stomach was bare, taut muscles delighting her hungry eyes, and pointed strips of obsidian edged with gold encircled his lean hips over a black loincloth, barely protecting his modesty.

Something that she was lacking.

She forced her gaze onwards, taking in the toned length of his legs, from his muscular thighs to the plates that protected his shins. They were as powerful as the rest of him.

Her eyes roamed back up, over the black cuffs that covered his forearms, decorated in gold with images of lions, and over his bare biceps to his strong shoulders. From there, they wanted to go to his face, but his wings were too fascinating. They were huge, casting a shadow across both him and her despite the fact they were tucked against his back.

She wanted to walk around him and investigate every delicious inch of him, taking in that he really was an angel and not a man parading as one.

An angel.

Abaddon.

Her mother had taught her gods, goddesses and mythology. She knew all about him and his kind.

Her eyes finally leaped to his face, a need to see in his vivid blue eyes that he was telling the truth racing through her again. She found the reassurance she needed, together with something else to fascinate her. He had flecks of paler blue, like ice, in his irises.

His lips tilted at the corners, and she had the strangest sensation that her appraisal was making him nervous. He didn't show it though. His gaze held hers, unwavering and strong, and her temperature rose as his eyes narrowed slightly and his pupils dilated.

What was he thinking in there?

Did he like what he saw as much as she did?

The man was a god.

No, an angel.

And he was beautiful.

Breathtaking.

But he wasn't at all as she had thought an angel would look. Everything about him spoke of darkness, right down to his aura. Whatever power he had, it was strong and it wasn't the sort that resurrected mortals or healed them. It felt as though the opposite would happen if he unleashed it.

Abaddon. The angel of death. Although he had denied that title. What title did he claim as his then?

"So, Abaddon—" she started.

"Apollyon," he interjected with a charming smile that teased his sensual lips and made her heart beat a little faster.

He was an angel. Serenity reminded herself of that ten times over and then once more to make it stick.

It didn't matter how good he looked, or how he was making her forget her pain just by looking at him, she couldn't think about him like that. It was wrong of her. He had offered his assistance in getting revenge on her bastard ex and she was going to take it. Whatever dark power this gorgeous man had, she was going to let it rip in her ex's direction and reclaim her dignity and her property.

"Apollyon?" She barely stopped her gaze from dropping down to take him in again.

If she told him to put on something a little less distracting, would he be able to do it? She had seen through whatever spell he had used. Could he ever fool her eyes?

"I prefer my true name." He cast a quick glance over her.

His eyes lingered in all the places a mortal man's would and flames ignited in her blood, making it burn and threatening to turn all of her restraint to ashes. She cleared her throat, causing his eyes to leap back up to meet hers, and reined in her wicked feelings.

The banked heat in his eyes lingered, making her question everything.

Surely, she was off limits too? Angels were asexual, weren't they? Androgynous? Whatever the one was that meant he had no sexual feelings. Zero libido.

The voice at the back of her mind said that the tall hunk of handsome standing in front of her definitely didn't look asexual or androgynous. He looked like sin incarnate, not like an angel at all.

"Serenity." She offered her hand to him.

He took it and a jolt ran through her the moment his strong hand engulfed hers. She quickly shook his hand but he didn't let go when she was done. He held it, his thumb resting lightly against hers.

"My mother thought I could bring peace to a chaotic world," she said absently, her heart thundering as she stared at his thumb. It grazed hers, stroked it in a way that sent a hot shiver tripping through her and had those wicked thoughts returning. She tried to banish them, fought to focus on anything but him. He made it impossible when he took his hand back, his fingers brushing her palm and sending another shiver through her. "I'm not much good at it."

"At what?" He quirked a dark eyebrow and tilted his head to one side.

Serenity sighed inside. Did he know how good he looked? Could angels be conceited? She supposed they were all beautiful so he probably didn't realise that the reason all the women were staring as they passed wasn't because they thought he was apprehending her or anything of the sort.

They were staring for the same reason she was.

The man was six feet plus of godliness.

"Being peaceful... I'm actually quite chaotic." She shrugged. "Nothing I do comes out right. I mean... I thought I was casting a simple spell for vengeance and suddenly you're here telling me that you heard me calling you. I wasn't asking for an angel."

"You weren't." He placed his palm flat against her chest and she jumped. Her pulse rocketed and she blushed from head to toe at the feel of his wrist against her breasts. "Your heart called me, not your words."

Serenity smiled, caught hold of his hand with trembling fingers and removed it from her chest before she lost control and threw herself at him.

"So you're good with revenge?" She released his hand, ignoring the buzz that lingered, vibrating in her chest in the spot where his hand had been.

"Very good at it." He stood taller, straightening to his full impressive height, looking even more noble and handsome. "I am Apollyon, the great destroyer, king of the bottomless—"

"Wait." She held her hands up. "Great destroyer? Maybe this isn't such a good idea. I mean, you're an angel and your boss-on-high would probably be a little upset if you blew up half of Paris to fulfil my wish for revenge, and I don't want him dead... just in pain... and I can really take care of this myself. I didn't mean to bother you."

"It is little bother." He frowned. "I will only do as you command. The choice of revenge will be yours and I will exact it."

"What about your boss?" She didn't want to piss God off.

No more than she probably already did anyway.

Most witches she had met believed that whatever higher power existed, it was fairly angry that people like them existed on Earth, those that could use magic and make their own miracles.

Not that she had managed anything like that so far. She was better at lighting candles and the small stuff like love potions. Her life as a witch was one big cliché, but it paid the bills.

Serenity glanced up at Apollyon. Would a love potion work on an angel?

She cursed and told herself to get a grip. Angels probably couldn't enter into relationships with mortals and this attraction to him was purely because she was rebounding, and she was rebounding hard. What better way to get over a man than to find another one? She shook that thought away. It wasn't her style. None of this was.

Maybe she should just put an end to this before it began and send him home, wherever that was.

"You are my master now." The serious edge to his expression said that he wasn't joking. "I do as you bid."

Serenity's eyebrows rose as she slowly absorbed the fact that she had her own personal angel and the thought of telling him to go home drifted into the background.

Maybe just a little revenge.

She did need to get her property back after all.

It was humiliating enough that her ex had cheated on her, the fact he had stolen two of her coven's most precious spell books from her was just… there were no words. If she didn't get them back before her coven discovered they were gone, she was going to be in serious trouble.

Her coven already thought she was more than useless and dead weight. The only reason she had been invited was because of her family name. They would kick her out if they got wind of what had happened and she couldn't let that happen. She couldn't dishonour her family like that.

"Then we should..." She wasn't sure what they should do. Skulk off and plan something horrible to do to her ex because he had cheated on her? It all felt a little cloak and dagger and not at all like her. She had never sworn revenge on anyone, had always let her anger go and just got on with her life. Not this time though. She wanted him to pay. "Do you drink coffee?"

"I have never tried it." Apollyon smiled. "But I have been told by others that it tastes strangely bitter and sweet at the same time, and has an interesting effect on the body. I would like to try it."

"Coffee it is." Serenity led the way towards the fountains and glanced across at Apollyon as he fell into step beside her.

She really hoped that people weren't seeing him as she was.

"What do you look like to them?" She looked at a few people to make her point.

"A man dressed in a black suit."

"No wings?"

He shook his head. "Do not worry. It is only you who are unaffected by the image I project."

"Can it affect me?"

He stopped and looked at her. The breeze tousled his fine long black hair, teasing the strands of his ponytail and causing them to flutter over his left shoulder.

"You wish not to see me as I am?" His dark eyebrows pinched, and a hint of something filled his eyes, something that looked a lot like displeasure.

Or perhaps disappointment.

When he said it like that, it made her feel bad. His blue eyes darted between hers, as though he wanted to see the answer in them before she said it.

"No." She stepped towards him, her heart beating faster again as her palms sweated, and drew down a deep breath before smiling up at him. "You're fine just the way you are."

The wind blew again, catching her blonde hair and sweeping it across her face.

She tensed when he brushed the strands from her face, smoothing them behind her ear, and his fingertips caressed her cheek as he trailed his hand off her.

Did he know what he did to her with that touch? What just looking at him did to her on the inside?

She kept telling herself that he was an angel and he was off limits, but her body wasn't getting the message. It burned to feel his hands on it, to feel his lips against hers and have him hold her close.

Which was insane.

She had only just met him and she wasn't the sort who threw herself at men. Her ex, Edward, had pursued her for months before she had finally given in and agreed to a date with him, let alone anything else.

Now she was ready to throw herself into the arms of an angel and pray that he caught her and kissed her just as she wanted him to.

"He really hurt you," Apollyon whispered.

Serenity blinked and her desire deflated at the thought of what Edward had done to her. She really had to clear her head of whatever ridiculous attraction she felt to Apollyon because it wasn't going to happen.

He was an angel.

This time, she reminded herself of that fact one hundred times and then once more.

She started walking again, not waiting for him to follow because she needed a moment to breathe.

Since setting eyes on him, her head and heart had been at war and it was time she gave both of them a reality check.

Apollyon was here to help her get revenge and that was all.

She couldn't throw herself at him, or make a move, or do anything that would only end in her getting her heart broken again or winding up as miserable as Edward had made her.

"I said something wrong?" Apollyon strode beside her, his long lithe legs making easy work of her hurried pace.

She was quiet a moment, lost in her thoughts and unable to find her voice as her gaze drifted over the pale stone buildings that lined the narrow street.

"No." She moved through the crowd at a busy intersection, crossed the road and then walked along another narrow road to the street where her favourite café was. "It just caught me off guard. I mean, I get this sense that you know what you're talking about... as though you... it's silly."

"Can feel it?" he offered.

She stopped dead outside the café and looked back at him.

He stood a few paces behind her, his black wings still tucked against his back and the gold decoration on his obsidian armour reflecting the sun.

She nodded.

He walked up to her and looked down into her eyes. "I *can* feel it. It is part of the reason I agreed to help you. You do not deserve such pain. You always seemed so happy until recently."

Always seemed so happy?

Wait.

"You've been *spying* on me?" It came out louder than she had intended.

A pair of well-dressed dark-haired women sitting at one of the round dark metal tables in front of the café looked her way and then started talking in hushed voices.

"I am an ang—" He frowned when Serenity slapped her hand over his mouth.

His warm breath bathed her skin, tickling her and sending a shiver dancing up her arm, rousing those wicked thoughts she kept trying to vanquish.

Serenity snatched her hand back. "I don't think that's a good word to use in public."

"We all watch. It is what we do."

She grimaced. That had probably sounded even worse. The two women were deep in conversation now, furtively glancing at her and Apollyon. They probably thought she had a harem of stalkers.

Serenity grabbed Apollyon's hand and dragged him into the small café. It was quieter inside, only a few people at the round wooden tables and in the armchairs. She chose a spot away from everyone, near the window, and sat Apollyon down in a low brown armchair next to a small table.

"Wait here," she said and hoped that he would.

What had she gotten herself into?

She should have sent him away. She shouldn't have allowed herself to get caught up in the idea of revenge and the hope of regaining the coven's property before they realised it had been taken from her.

She needed her coven though.

All witches did.

They were an extension of her family and the thought they might kick her out left her cold inside. Not only because her family would be disappointed, but because she had passed so many happy years with her coven, had learned so much from them and had made friends there.

So, damn it, no matter what happened, she was willing to do whatever it took to get the books back and prevent her coven from kicking her out.

Even making a deal with an angel.

Serenity ordered the coffees and looked over at Apollyon while she waited for them to come. His cerulean eyes remained locked on the world outside, a soft edge to his expression that looked a lot like longing to her.

Watching the world go by? Did angels really do that? If he said they did, then they probably did all watch over the mortals.

He shifted his shoulders, frowned and then his black wings unfurled, sending a breeze through the room that had people grabbing their papers, napkins and anything else that had tried to escape in the wind.

Serenity stared open-mouthed at the sight of him. He sat with his black feathered wings outstretched behind him, almost reaching back to the other side of the room. How big was his wingspan? Each wing had to be at least ten foot long.

She grabbed the coffees when they arrived, went back to him, and sat in a daze in the armchair opposite him, staring at his wings.

Apollyon shifted his shoulders and his wings furled again, the longest feathers curling around and grazing his boots.

"I needed to stretch," he said with an apologetic look and then smiled. "It has been a long time since I have had so much freedom. It feels good to stretch my wings."

She bet it did. He looked like the cat that got the cream, smiling ear to ear, a twinkle in his blue eyes.

"What does it feel like to fly?" The words had left her lips before she could even consider what she was asking.

His smile widened. "Bliss. The wind on my face, the feel of it in my feathers, and the way I can see everything and go anywhere. There is no feeling like it."

"It sounds nice. I've flown... in a plane... but it's still flying, right? Something in common."

"Would you like to fly?" He canted his head again, a dash of curiosity lighting his eyes as he studied her.

Was he offering to take her up? The thought made her stomach feel tight but something inside her made her nod.

"I am sure we can do something about it." He picked up the white mug of coffee and raised a dark eyebrow at it.

He sniffed it first, peered at the frothy top, and then took a sip.

His feathers quivered and his eyes widened, darting to hers. "What drug is in this?"

Serenity picked up her own mug of latte and sipped. "It's not really a drug. It's caffeine, a natural stimulant. Humans are addicted to it."

He eyed the mug suspiciously. "A stimulant?"

He looked as though he was going to take another sip and then set it back down on the round table between them. His gaze met hers again and his pupils dilated until his irises were almost as black as them. He shifted uncomfortably and crossed his legs, settling his hands in his lap.

"I do not think I should drink any more. It would be unwise." His voice was tight and the unmistakable spark of desire in his eyes wasn't going anywhere. "I will be having words with my fellow warriors when we next meet. They did not explain the effects well enough."

Effects? She looked down at his hands in his lap and then back into his dark eyes.

Viagra for angels?

"I thought you were all asexual," she blurted and then covered her mouth when he turned horrified eyes on her.

She blushed ten shades of crimson and tried to think of a spell that would take back what she had said. It probably wouldn't work on him anyway. Magic didn't affect gods and goddesses, so it was unlikely to affect other supernatural beings.

"I am not asexual." The way he said that made it clear that he would be happy to prove it to her right now in the coffee shop.

Serenity gulped her drink and kept her focus on it, avoiding the smouldering look he was giving her and wanting to crawl under the table and hide.

"I have not had a woman in many centuries but I am in no way an impotent creature."

Did he have to say it loud enough for the whole coffee shop to hear? She sunk into her chair, trying to avoid the looks she was getting.

"I take it back," she whispered into her mug and peered at him over the rim of it.

He glowered, passion no longer reigning in his eyes. A dark malevolence shone there and the sense that he wasn't exactly a good angel in the way she had imagined them returned.

"Some people say you're the Devil," she whispered.

He leaned back into his chair and sighed. "First I am the angel of death, and now the Devil? The rumours do spread and stick, don't they?"

"What are you then?" She emerged from her mug, sat forwards on the edge of the armchair seat and looked him over.

He was sin made flesh, that was what he was, luscious in every way imaginable, and she was sure that angels weren't supposed to be so tempting.

"I told you. Apollyon, the great destroyer... angel of the Apocalypse, responsible for raining hell down on Earth when everything comes to an end."

That wasn't comforting at all.

"You're not a good angel then?" She hoped he would say that he was, that he was merely teasing her and she hadn't just summoned a very dangerous warrior to do her bidding.

He smiled and there was a sexy sort of darkness in his look. "I am good, if by that you mean I do not work for the Devil, but I can be very bad."

She could imagine. She shouldn't be, but she was picturing him in every position possible and he looked wicked from every angle.

"So what does my mistress command?" His smile held and something about it made her feel as though he was encouraging her to say the things that were raging through her head.

What didn't she want to command?

She couldn't though. She was sure that it was wrong to order an angel to commit sin. For now, while her conscience was still functioning and she could resist the temptation sitting across from her, she would focus on getting her revenge.

"Nothing involving death. I want him to suffer. I want him to feel jealous and hurt and unloved... as though he doesn't matter to me." Her voice gained a bitter edge as those words left her, stirred anger in her that rolled back to a swift boil, as potent as it had been the night she had realised what Edward had done to her.

Apollyon smiled as though he liked the sound of that.

She held his blue gaze.

What she was going to propose was crazy and there was a danger it would shatter what little restraint she had around him, but she was going to do it.

"I have a plan."

# CHAPTER 4

Apollyon perfected his image, smoothing his long black hair back into his neat ponytail and tightening the knot of his blue tie. Warmth rolled off the sandstone buildings that lined the elegant shopping avenue and the trees growing at intervals close to the busy road to his right swayed softly in the breeze, mingling with the hum of the cars. The golden light from the store windows washed over his left side, and the lamps made his and Serenity's shadows dance as they walked.

He studied every little thing, struggling to focus on his mission. So much about this world fascinated him, tugged at his natural curiosity and kept trying to distract him.

Serenity remained quiet beside him, distant and lost in her own thoughts. Was she worried about her plan?

It was simple, yet likely to be effective.

He glanced across at her, taking in how different she looked in the short black sleeveless dress that hugged her breasts and flared out from her waist, and the black high heels. She had tied her blonde hair up into a loose chignon, and dark kohl now lined her eyes and her lips were stained red, adding to her allure.

It had been difficult not to look at her before, but now it was impossible.

She drew his eyes to her every second he was in her presence and he didn't want to look away.

He wanted to stare at her forever.

He reminded himself that it was alright now. He was supposed to look at her, to be attentive and charming, to be romantic with her.

"He'll be here." The tremble in her voice betrayed the nerves he could easily feel in her.

Was she having second thoughts? Her form of revenge was far more gentle and lenient than the one he would have chosen for the man she called Edward, a bastard who had not only betrayed her but had apparently stolen precious items from her too, heirlooms that belonged to her clan.

For such sins, he would happily cast the wretched mortal into the bottomless pit to suffer there and let the Devil and his legion of demonic angels have their way with him.

Her heartbeat quickened, dragging him away from pleasing thoughts of watching her unfaithful lover suffer.

He looked ahead, following her gaze, and spotted the illuminated sign of the club she had mentioned to him, one she had frequented with his target and one popular with witches.

It was sandwiched between two stores, the windows on either side of the glass doors blacked out. Elegant lamps mounted on the sandstone wall on either side of the door cast a warm glow over the bustling queue hemmed in behind a black velvet rope suspended between gold metal posts and small groups of mortals who had gathered to talk and smoke together on the pavement.

Apollyon's gaze flickered over everyone, singling out those who had power. He had yet to get a description of his target, hadn't had the heart to press her for one when she had clammed up and said she was having second thoughts. She had promised to point Edward out to him though.

"I shouldn't be asking you to do this." Serenity stopped and turned to face him, and he wanted to sigh as he realised they were going to do this again. "It's really not right."

"You are only asking me to pretend that I am your new lover. It will be an easy charade, and it will not contravene any law of the contract that lies between us." He smiled at her, hoping it would alleviate her nerves and convince her to continue with their plan.

She nodded and he kept the truth to himself, felt wretched for concealing it from her but it was necessary. If she knew it, she would send him away, would refuse to go through with things.

Nothing could contravene the laws of their contract.

Because he hadn't invited her to create any or made any of his own.

Whatever she desired of him, she would have.

Sin or no sin involved.

And he was fine with that.

Serenity moved closer to him and he bit back the groan that rolled up his throat as her light perfume teased his senses with its floral notes, luring him to her as much as her appearance. He had forgotten how good females smelled.

Damn, the scent of her fired him up, had him perilously close to forgetting his duty and his mission, forgetting everything but her.

Dangerous. She was dangerous and he knew it, but he didn't care.

Something about this beautiful, enchanting female had him bewitched, utterly entranced by her.

She went to move away but he snagged her wrist, unwilling to let her move away. She stopped, glanced at his hand on her and then lifted her beautiful hazel eyes to meet his.

"You are nervous." He grazed his fingertips over her skin, enjoying the silky warm feel of her.

Whenever he touched her, he didn't want to let her go. No. He couldn't bring himself to let her go. It was impossible. He wanted to run his hands over every inch of her and feel the subtle differences across her body, studying her and memorising every supple plane and curve.

"You would be too if you were about to walk into a club with an angel on your arm." There was a hint of a joke about her tone but he knew that she was being serious.

His appearance to her disconcerted her.

"I do not look like an angel to mortals, and I believe you have a particular gift that allows you to see through my glamour, one the other witches are unlikely to share." He took hold of her shoulders and turned her to face the dark window of the shop behind her.

Her eyes widened.

Whatever ability she had, she evidently couldn't see through an illusion he cast on something else. He was projecting his image onto his reflection, so she would see what other mortals did when they looked at him.

"You look like that?"

He nodded, leaned forwards until his chest was close to her shoulders, almost grazing her back, and looked down at her face.

"Does my reflection satisfy you?" He studied her profile, found himself eager to know whether it did.

She looked at him over her shoulder, her face close to his. "I think I prefer to see you as you are."

The honesty in those words touched his heart.

His gaze fell to her lips and he stepped back, away from the temptation they presented.

"You have taste though," she said and he looked back at her. "In suits and in armour."

Apollyon smiled. "If you are satisfied, then let us begin your revenge."

He held his hand out to her, only meaning for her to take it as a hint to go to the club rather than for her to hold it but she slipped hers into it. Her hand was small in his, delicate, and he stared down at them as he walked with her to the club, a strange but powerful sense of possessiveness rolling through him, making him burn with a need to protect her.

Had he ever held someone's hand before?

If he had, it was too long ago to recall and it couldn't have felt this good. He wouldn't have forgotten it if it had.

The man on the door, a mortal dressed in a sharp black suit with neatly styled dark hair, stepped aside the moment they neared and Serenity looked across at Apollyon.

He shrugged. Some mortals were easier to compel than others. The bouncer had been an easy target. A message sent straight into the man's head saying that he wanted to let the beautiful woman pass had been enough to make him lift the black velvet rope for them.

Apollyon led her through the brightly-lit foyer where more people were milling around. She moved in front of him, leading him towards another set of doors. The heavy beat of music filled the air, distant and quiet, more of a feeling vibrating in his chest than a noise.

That all changed when she pushed one of the double doors open.

He flinched as the volume of the music hit him but kept following her, into the darker interior of the club.

His eyes adjusted as he moved forwards and he looked around, taking note of everything about his surprisingly elegant surroundings. Gold neon lit a black bar ahead of him, white spotlights casting pale light over the bartenders and the patrons gathered there. Mirrors backed the shelves of colourful bottles behind the bar, an entire rainbow of alcohol that the people packed into the nightclub seemed bent on consuming as they hollered orders at the bartenders.

He studied the well-dressed people, singling out those with power. There were more than he had anticipated, and he had the feeling not all of them were witches.

Serenity tugged him deeper into the club as he scanned the mortals. The dance floor was small and busy with people performing what he could only interpret as clothed sex. Blue strobes and lasers made their movements stuttered and broken as they gyrated against each other.

At the edges of the room, clusters of tall round black tables with gold edging surrounded by black velvet stools filled the space. Most of them were occupied, with some groups having dragged over stools from other tables, or moved the tables themselves to form enough room for their entire party. They spoke loudly to each other, fighting to be heard over the volume of the music. If he could call it music.

The fast hard beat made him actually miss the relative peace of Hell.

Serenity suddenly stopped and he bumped into the back of her.

The feel of her warm body against his front stirred him as badly as the coffee had done and he backed off a step so she wouldn't notice. She looked over her shoulder at him and motioned with her eyes towards the dance floor.

If she expected him to be able to pick out Edward from a crowd, she was overestimating his abilities.

She took hold of his arm and he felt her fingers against his skin rather than the jacket of his suit. She could reach through his glamour too. He burned where she touched, growing hungry for more, for her to touch other parts of him.

He was starting to see why some of his fellow warriors had pledged themselves to mortal women.

Had those under his command, the small band of warriors he had come to feel were his friends, bound by their history and a companionship that had lasted millennia, found females of their own?

He hadn't heard from the group in a long time, blamed Hell for his absence in their lives and theirs in his. Many of them couldn't enter the realm, were unable to get permission to venture there.

One of them had entered Hell never to return.

He had long thought Rook dead, extinguished from existence somehow even when he had hoped the guardian angel had been sent back to Heaven to be reborn and reassigned to a different group. The arrival of Marcus in their team had given rise to that hope, but all the years Apollyon had passed in Heaven, he had never seen Rook.

Now, he knew Rook had suffered a fate worse than death.

Apollyon still couldn't shake how he had felt when a battalion of demonic angels had come to the plateau in response to several of their foul breed attempting to goad him into a fight and he had seen the one who commanded them.

Rook.

It had been centuries or more since he had seen the male last, but he had easily recognised him. He had trained the angel, had been close enough to him to consider him a friend, and was bound to him via a connection so strong that not even death could sever it. Rook had been part of his team, the angel from the guardian corps in his elite squad formed of one warrior from each faction.

Rook had been closest to Einar, the hunter, and had teased Lukas, the mediator, as badly as the rest of them.

While he had recognised Rook, the male hadn't recognised him.

He'd had so many questions to ask him, but before he could voice any of them, the entire battalion had moved on, and he hadn't seen Rook again since then.

How would Lukas and Einar react if they knew Rook was alive? If they knew he had fallen?

He twisted so he could see the door of the nightclub through the crowd, a pressing need to go and tell his brethren what he had discovered pounding in him. He was on Earth now. He could find his way back to them through the bond they shared and tell them what had happened to Rook. Maybe they could find a way to convince Rook to return to Heaven.

Although, that meant convincing him to die.

Only through death could Rook be reborn as an angel of Heaven again.

Serenity's palm brushing his biceps pulled him back to her and he returned his focus to her, silently vowing to find the others and let them know that Rook had fallen.

She tiptoed, her breasts pressing against his arm and his chest, completely destroying his ability to focus on anything but the way they felt against him, and the intense need for more that flooded him.

She pulled on his arm, tugging him downwards, and he lowered his ear to her mouth when he finally clawed back enough sense to realise that she wanted to say something to him.

"The mousy-haired man, white shirt, exposing far too much chest," she shouted into his ear and he grimaced.

He should have told her that he had sensitive hearing.

He looked for his target, gaze scanning the dancers, and zeroed in when he spotted him. Serenity was right, and the male was showing far too much chest. His white shirt had at least the top three buttons undone.

Apollyon's gaze shifted to Edward's companion, a slender dark-haired woman in a revealing tight pale dress.

"Is that the female he betrayed you with?" He frowned.

The woman was nothing compared with Serenity. His gaze dropped to her and she shook her head.

What sort of womaniser had Serenity been involved with? The thought of her with such a man made him desire to change plans and send him to Hell after all, and maybe the demonic angels and the Devil wouldn't be the only ones making him suffer.

"Do you want a drink?" she shouted over the noise of the music.

Apollyon shook his head. "I do not think alcohol would be wise. I have not tasted it before and I am not sure whether it is still forbidden."

Serenity looked past him to the bar. "Well, I need a drink."

"Then a drink you will have." He released her hand. "I will be just a moment."

He heard her gasp when he disappeared. A woman looked right at him when he appeared in a space next to her, accidently knocking against her, and he smiled his apology. The anger that had been in her dark eyes disappeared in an instant.

"Can I buy you a drink, Handsome?" She fluttered her long lashes at him and smiled.

He had never been in the game but he knew when a woman was flirting. He looked over towards Serenity where she stood by the dance floor, staring through the crowd at him, shock still written across her face.

"I am here with someone." He sensed the woman's gaze leave him.

She snorted. "Really, you ought to trade up."

Was she insinuating that Serenity wasn't good enough for him and that perhaps she was?

He laughed. He had never heard something so ridiculous. Why would he want to leave Serenity for the woman before him? Serenity was kind, warm, he looked back at her and his smile slowly fell as it began to dawn on him, and beautiful.

She really was beautiful.

And he wanted her.

# CHAPTER 5

That revelation hit Apollyon hard.

He had never wanted a mortal woman before, not like this. This was want. Need. It consumed and controlled him, flooded him with an urge to return to her, to touch her because he craved the feel of her beneath his fingers, ached constantly to be close to her.

He flagged down the bartender and compelled him to make the same brightly coloured drink as the flirtatious woman had in front of her. The man made it and slid the martini glass across the bar to him. Apollyon took it and left, disappearing and reappearing beside Serenity.

She gasped again and then smiled when he held the drink out to her.

"I am not sure what it is."

"Did your new friend recommend it?" She was still smiling but there was something different about her.

Something darker that came with a strong sense of power.

Jealous?

"She recommended something else and I refused." He offered the drink again and Serenity took it this time, moved the small black straws around so the ice clinked against the sides of the glass and then sucked on them.

Apollyon stared at her mouth, mesmerised as she removed the straws and licked her lips.

"Good?" he said and she nodded.

The power that had radiated from her disappeared and she smiled. It had been a long time since he had dealt with a witch. Was she strong enough to curse him? He wasn't sure if his own powers would stand against hers and he didn't want to find out.

Just thinking about it had his thoughts returning to Rook. A witch had been his downfall.

Now that Apollyon was looking back, now that Serenity had awoken feelings and desires in him, perhaps the witch hadn't been Rook's downfall.

He was starting to feel it had been love.

Rook had fallen in love with the witch he had been assigned to protect. A witch who had been captured and dragged to Hell, and one Apollyon was beginning to believe was dead, because what else would have caused Rook to fall?

He looked at Serenity and felt the full force of his desire for her and the feelings that were growing behind that veil of need and hunger, of lust. A question rang in his mind, one that left him cold because he couldn't answer it straight away.

If this witch was taken from him, if the Devil dragged her down to Hell and killed her before him, would he fall just as Rook had?

He wasn't sure he would be strong enough to go on, to let the rage it would ignite in him burn out and continue with his life as an angel, unaffected by the loss. He wasn't sure he would be able to hold back that rage and stop himself from waging war against all of Hell.

"Apollyon?" Serenity moved closer to him, her fair eyebrows furrowing as she gazed up at him and a flicker of concern in her hazel eyes. "Is something wrong?"

He forced a smile and shook his head, but it was another lie, because everything was wrong. Everything was changing and he couldn't keep up, not with the world that closed in around him or with the feelings rushing to life inside him.

The table nearest them became free and he placed his hand against her elbow, guiding her over to it, because he needed to sit for a moment so he could get his head on straight again and find his feet.

She slid onto the tall black velvet stool and placed her drink down on the round black table.

Apollyon sat opposite her, watching her sip her drink and waiting for the world to stop tilting and swaying and feeling as if at any moment it was all going to drop from under him.

The music continued to pound but soon changed to a new song. Some of the dancers left the floor and walked past them towards the bar. Serenity stiffened, her heart beating faster as she paused midway through sipping her drink.

He brought his focus back to her and the club, pushing out the conflict that was trying to drag him down into a dark abyss, and frowned as he sensed the male she had pointed out closing in on them.

Apollyon reached across the table and placed his hand over Serenity's just as Edward reached them.

He smiled at her when he felt Edward's focus settle on them, sensed the male's agitation and surprise, and then glared at the bastard's back as he moved away. Everything that was dark in him, all of the parts he did his best to suppress and control, goaded him into following and dealing with the man, whispered tempting things about meting out justice and making him pay.

Serenity's hand shifted beneath his and her eyes were enormous when he dragged his away from Edward's back and settled them on her.

"Did he see?" She leaned towards him, affording him a glorious view down her black dress to her breasts.

Was she trying to tempt him?

"He saw." Apollyon peered over the crowd, tracking Edward's progress across the room.

Edward was shorter than him, and his build was slighter. He seemed plain in the face but it was difficult to tell in such poor light. The male had to have some good qualities to draw Serenity to him and make her care for him. Right now though, Apollyon couldn't see anything good in him. He saw only a sinner, a man to be punished and made to suffer, just as his mistress desired.

Edward reached the bar and looked back at him.

No, at them. He was looking at them. He would have seen that Serenity was with him and that they were more than just friends.

Serenity sipped her drink again and Apollyon grazed his thumb lightly over the back of her hand, staring at them. She didn't seem to mind him touching her, or was it all part of the act?

His gaze rose to her face, studying her as she sucked on the two small black straws. Her blonde hair shone blue in the lights and the cold colour of them washed out her skin and made her make-up even darker.

She looked up from her drink and released the straws. Her smile teased him, curving her dark lips and tempting him to take this charade further just to see how she would react.

"What sort of spells can you cast?" he said over the music.

She slowly stirred her drink with the straws, staring into his eyes the whole time. Did she have to think that hard about it? Could she cast spells on men that made them her willing slave? If she could, he would swear that she had cast one on him.

"My mother told me only to do magic that benefitted others, and I had until today." She lifted the glass to her lips, pushed the straws aside, and took a long gulp of the drink. She set the empty glass down. "I've done minor curses for people, spells to aid maternity and conception, and love spells of course."

Love spells.

Perhaps she had cast that spell on him.

She had never used magic to benefit herself before today.

He had seen enough of the world to know that she was unusual in that respect. Her warmth, her selflessness and kindness, spoke to his heart, making her more beautiful. She thought only of helping others when most who possessed her powers would use them to profit from other humans. Power was a drug to mortals. He had seen the effect it had on them. Another person with her abilities would have used it to make them rich, important and popular, lured in by the promises of false happiness it gave until they were addicted to it.

Serenity seemed immune to it, and when she had finally succumbed to using it for herself, it had been to heal the pain in her heart and have vengeance. The hurt her ex-lover had caused her had driven her to use her power.

And Apollyon had heard her call and responded.

Perhaps he was the result of her spell after all. Her magic could have amplified her voice and he could have heard it because his focus had been on her at the time.

"You are never tempted to use them?" He leaned closer to her, unsure how many of the people coming and going past them were witches and not wanting any normal humans in the area to overhear their conversation.

She shook her head and then glanced away. "Perhaps sometimes."

Sometimes.

Her gaze snuck back to him, meeting his, and her cheeks darkened. It would have been impossible to see it if he hadn't been watching for it. She had considered a spell. On who? On Edward or on him? Revenge or love?

Serenity's other hand settled over their joined ones. It was cold from holding the glass but soon warmed on contact with his skin. She turned the hand that was beneath his, trapping his between hers.

"Do you think we should dance?" There was a nervous edge to her expression as her gaze flickered past him, over his shoulder.

"Is he still watching?" Apollyon could already feel the man's gaze on him.

She nodded.

"Then we should definitely dance."

She hesitated. "Is it okay to dance... to do any of this?"

How many times was she going to ask him the same question?

His answer wasn't going to change.

Whatever she wanted, he would do it.

He was starting to think he would do more than she asked if she showed him again that she desired him, that this attraction wasn't one sided and he wasn't the only one feeling things.

Apollyon took hold of her hand, stood and walked around the table to her. His smile seemed to give her the answer that she was looking for, bringing another dark blush to her cheeks, and she slipped from her stool and followed his lead towards the dance floor.

The music was heavier now, harder, and slower. The dancers were bordering on clothed sex again and, for a moment, he wondered if it really was a good idea. He wasn't sure where a dance would lead, but the heat in Serenity's eyes as he risked a glance at her told him that wherever it took them, it wasn't pretend.

He wasn't the only one feeling this attraction, this gravity that seemed intent on pulling him towards her.

He tugged her into his arms before his nerve failed. Her hands landed on his chest, scalding him despite his armour, and he forgot what he had been doing and ended up standing stock still and staring down into her wide eyes.

Her pupils dilated, devouring the hazel of her irises, until her eyes overflowed with the passion and hunger that he could feel beating in her heart.

The same passion and hunger that drummed in his veins.

Whenever she let go of her nerves and of the fact that he was an angel, she was more confident, sensual in her movements and almost flirtatious in her air around him. He wanted her like that now, and not because it would make Edward jealous to see it.

But because he needed it.

He needed to know that whatever she had felt for Edward, it was over. Done. He needed to know that she felt something for him.

Apollyon slid his hands down to her waist from her ribs, and over her hips. She felt too good beneath his touch. He wanted to caress every inch of her, wanted to learn her curves and every sensitive spot on her body. He wanted to bring her to life in the way she had brought him to life, flooding him with feelings that were foreign to him now, startling in their strength and how easily they overwhelmed him.

Her eyelids slipped to half-mast and her palms pressed harder against his chest, not on his suit but on his armour. Did she like the feel of his hands on her? Was she enjoying this tentative exploration as much as he was?

He tightened his grip on her hips and drew her against him, starting to move slowly to the heavy beat because he was meant to be dancing with her, and he feared that if he didn't start now, he never would and she would question him again, might even pull away from him. He wasn't sure he could handle that, not when he was loving the feel of her in his arms.

Her hands slid up over his breastplate and then over his collarbones towards his neck, and he shivered when she lightly swept her fingers across his shoulders, teasing the straps of his armour. He fell back under her spell again as she stepped into him, bringing their bodies into contact, and began moving against his.

Each time they brushed, each step that had them rubbing against each other, drove him a little closer to the edge of control.

Serenity didn't help when she slipped her hands around the back of his head, twirled the dark hair of his ponytail around her slender fingers, and then settled them against the nape of his neck.

He shifted his trembling hands, easing them around her back, until they met in the small of it and she was flush against him. He bit back a groan at the feel of the way her hips moved as she danced with him, how her leg would slide between his and his between hers.

When his thigh brushed the apex of her thighs, her lips parted and her eyelids dropped to half-mast, a wickedly alluring glimmer of pleasure flitting across her face that made him want to press harder, to move closer.

He groaned aloud as he obeyed that need and moved closer to her, eager to feel the whole of her body against his, his thoughts diving down routes they hadn't traversed in a long time.

How good would she look naked?

He wanted to explore and tease every supple inch of her with his mouth and hands, wanted to worship her body until she cried his name and collapsed in his arms, sated by his touch.

His gaze dropped to her mouth.

How would she react if he kissed her?

Would she welcome it as part of the charade? Would she welcome it because she wanted to feel his lips on hers?

Or would she push him away?

Apollyon fought the urge to find out, struggled against it as she swayed in his arms, a tempting siren who was shredding his control with no more than a sultry swing of her hips and press of her thigh between his. He somehow found the strength to tamp it down and stepped back a little.

He needed a moment to breathe. He was too close to letting go.

Serenity stared into his eyes, hers full of invite, asking him to give in to her. He would do so willingly if he could be sure that this wasn't an act. It was a charade, nothing more than pretend so they would make Edward jealous. That was all it was.

So why did it feel so good to have her in his arms?

She ran her hands down over his biceps, slowly, her gaze following her right hand as it traced the curves of his muscles. Her heart beat faster, as though exploring his body excited her, and her eyes darkened again, hunger igniting in them that echoed in his veins.

Why did his body burn wherever she touched?

His gaze flickered to her mouth.

And why couldn't he keep his eyes off her cherry red lips and his mind off how good it would feel to dip his head and kiss her?

It had been a long time since he had desired a woman, but he knew it had never felt like this—so strong and irresistible. He loved how she moved against him, her body brushing his, teasing him into submission, sending shiver after shiver over his skin and sending his temperature soaring. He loved the way she looked into his eyes and smiled at him, so full of honest emotions and desire.

It didn't feel like an act.

It felt so real and he was sure that she would welcome a kiss from him.

It couldn't be the glamour because it didn't work on her. She had to be attracted to him.

She smiled up at him, her hands resting lightly by his elbows, burning him with her touch. He wanted to feel her hands on his chest but this time without his armour in the way. He needed her to touch him, to feel what she did to him and how hard she made his heart beat.

He moved against her, pressing closer again, satisfying himself as much as he could in public and without overstepping the mark. She didn't seem to care. Her eyes slipped shut when he ran his hands down to her backside and he groaned under his breath at the way the twin peachy globes moved beneath his fingers. He slid his hands lower, until he cupped her bottom, and drew her against him, so her hips were close to his.

He wanted her.

Her wide eyes met his, pupils swallowing her irises, and her lips parted.

He wanted to kiss her.

It couldn't be pretend.

He wanted to wrap her in his arms and his wings and never let her go.

What had she done to him?

What spell had she cast to make him like this?

Her fingertips caressed his arms, working back up to his shoulders, and she traced the line of the leather straps that held his armour in place. She toyed with the buckles, making his body tremble with the thought that he might get his wish and she might remove his breastplate and touch his bare chest.

He wanted that so much.

Her chest rose and fell with each hard breath, luring his eyes there. Deep hunger bolted through him at the sight of her breasts pressing against her small black dress and he lost track of what they were doing, until they were only holding each other, staring into each other's eyes, both of their hearts racing.

His gaze drifted back to her mouth and he couldn't fight the temptation.

Apollyon lowered his mouth towards hers, wrapped her in his arms, and tilted his head to kiss her.

She giggled.

He pulled back, frowning at her, confused as to her reaction. She thought his intent to kiss her was funny? She laughed then and wriggled against him, and he groaned low in his throat when her hip pressed against his aching erection.

She was beautiful when she laughed though, could laugh at him all she wanted and he wouldn't care, because it lit up her face and chased the clouds from her eyes. She brushed her shoulder and then down her arm, and he realised that it was his wings that had provoked her giggling fit.

He lifted one and swept the black feathers over her shoulder, and absorbed the way she burst into laughter in his arms. His lips curved into a smile as he watched her, warmth spreading through his entire body to lighten it.

She seemed to have forgotten her heartache.

They both seemed to have forgotten this was make believe.

# CHAPTER 6

Serenity stared up into Apollyon's dark eyes as he smiled down at her, seeing the passion and desire that burned deep within her reflected in them. She had to be imagining it. This was all just an act and it was working as far as she could tell, but then she had lost track of what Edward was doing the moment Apollyon had placed his hands on her.

The past few minutes had felt real.

They couldn't be.

His wings were a constant reminder of that and she had needed to feel them touching her to bring herself back to her senses. It didn't matter that he had looked as though he had been about to kiss her. He was an angel and he was definitely off limits.

Even if he did kiss her, she had to convince herself that it was only acting.

She couldn't fall for an angel, no matter how sexy the angel in question was. There was no hope of it becoming anything more than a mission to him. She wasn't naïve enough not to see that.

An angel couldn't fall in love with a mortal.

The song ended and Serenity looked over in the direction of Edward. He was gone. She looked around, tiptoeing to see over the heads of the crowd, and couldn't find him anywhere.

"He left." She took a step back from Apollyon.

Disappointment flashed across his handsome face as her hands slipped from him and she turned away so she didn't see it and could pretend that she had only imagined it.

Apollyon led her from the dance floor and went to sit down again at the table, but she caught his hand and headed for the exit instead.

There was no point in staying when Edward was gone. The music was giving her a headache and she had played pretend enough for a lifetime. When she had suggested it as a plan to get revenge on Edward, she hadn't considered the consequences or how it might affect her.

"We are leaving too?" Apollyon's deep voice did funny things to her insides and she wanted to be back in his arms, held close to him while he murmured sweet words into her ear.

Serenity nodded and quickly moved to the exit.

The cooling night air washed over her as she stepped out onto the pavement and she breathed deep of it as she tried to pull herself back together. She looked up, wishing she could see the stars. The sky was clear but the city lights caused a haze that blocked all but the brightest from view.

"You want to fly?" Those words were temptation, husked in a low voice close to her ear.

She ached to nod and throw caution to the wind. He moved closer to her, until she could feel his heat and a need to turn and kiss him until the fire he had ignited inside her burned out raced through her.

His breath tickled her neck as he lightly placed his hands on her shoulders, making her body warm and quake where his palms met her bare skin. "I can fly you home."

"I'm afraid of falling," she whispered.

Apollyon moved around her, sensual and like a predator, his gaze drilling into hers, as though he wanted to see right down into her heart and know the real meaning behind those words.

She *was* afraid.

She couldn't fall for an angel.

"I will not let you go." He claimed her waist and then stepped into her, sliding his hands around to settle in the arch of her back. His blue eyes held hers, the pale flecks of lightning in them mesmerising her. She could look into his eyes and never be bored. They shifted somehow. Each time the markings were slightly different, as though they were constantly changing. He smiled. "Would you prefer to face me or face away?"

Her pulse raced at the fiery heat in his look. Was she the only one masking the true meaning of their words or was he doing it too?

Serenity chided herself. An angel was hardly going to be asking about her sexual position preferences. She dragged her courage up from her toes, told herself that it was just a short flight to her apartment in the arms of a gorgeous dark angel, and that it was nothing more than that.

He raised an eyebrow when she looped her arms around his neck.

"I have a better idea." He scooped her up into his strong arms, cradling her there.

His armour was cool and hard against her side, but she didn't notice it as he held her close to him and his warm masculine scent filled her senses, tempting her to lean closer still, to do something reckless like resting her head on his shoulder, or maybe pressing a kiss to the oh-so-inviting patch of skin on his neck just below the strong line of his jaw.

How would he react if she did that?

The urge to find out was blasted from her mind when a breeze blew up her dress, chilling her bottom and pulling her back to reality. She raised her backside, grabbed the skirt of her black summer dress and tucked it in between her thighs. She didn't want to expose her bottom to the entirety of Paris.

Her eyebrows rose as she considered that. "Will people see us?"

Apollyon shook his head and looked up at the sky, his expression pensive. "They cannot see you now."

"You're hiding us?" She looked around and then at him.

He nodded and didn't give her a chance to ask how so she could assuage her curiosity about his powers.

He beat his huge black feathered wings and suddenly the world dropped out from under her.

She grabbed his shoulders and her eyes widened when she looked down, instantly regretting it when her stomach swirled as the ground zoomed away.

Serenity curled up against him, hiding her face against his neck as she gripped his armour so hard her hands hurt. Words rose to the tip of her tongue, a demand to set her back down again. She really didn't want to fall and she hadn't thought it through well enough.

What if he dropped her? What if she was too heavy?

Her eyes shot wide again and she pulled back, staring into his. "Are you sure your wings can carry both of us?"

He laughed, the timbre of it deep and warm, full of amusement that made her scowl.

"You weigh practically nothing." He squeezed her side and her knees where he held her. "Now which way?"

It took Serenity a moment to stop staring at him, stop absorbing how damned good he looked when he laughed and smiled, the whole of his face lighting up with it in a way that made her want to smile too.

She dragged her eyes away from him, because no good would come from staring at him, losing herself in him.

It was difficult to resist the urge to look back at him again, but she managed it by focusing on the task he had given her. Locating her apartment. Which was going to be easier said than done because it meant looking at the city, and she was sure the moment she saw the drop to it, her stomach was going to rebel and she was going to make a fool of herself.

She steeled herself by sucking down a few deep breaths to settle her stomach and then exhaled as she dropped her focus to the rooftops of Paris. Mercy, it was a long way down. Her eyes flitted over the city and she quickly pointed when she thought she had the right direction.

Apollyon swooped that way, his wings beating the cooler air, causing a breeze to tickle her skin.

She waited for her stomach to turn as they dropped, but it didn't. It remained calm as he flew with her.

She looked at the city for a moment, meaning only to glance before she hid again, but her breath left her in a rush as the sight of it hit her hard. It was beautiful. It stretched around her, a myriad of twinkling lights in the darkness, like a sea of stars beneath her.

Her gaze slid to Apollyon. He was incredible. She wished that she could fly like this. His focus stayed in the direction she had pointed, his grip on her sure, giving her comfort and confidence.

Making her realise something.

She trusted him.

It had been a long time since she had trusted someone so openly, so implicitly. She hadn't even trusted Edward this much. She barely knew Apollyon, but something about him felt right to her, as though they had been made for each other. Which was utterly ridiculous.

Apollyon looked at her, his eyes almost black in the low light, and she stilled in his arms, her heart beating steadily and slowly. He was so beautiful and dark. So tempting. Everything about him lit her up inside, had her trembling and weak, filled with needs that were startling in their intensity.

The strongest of which was a desire to never let him go.

He looked past her and then changed course with a hard beat of his wings. She curled up in his arms when he gained speed, plummeting towards the city, and was close to screaming until she saw the Eiffel Tower in the distance ahead, beautifully illuminated with white lights.

A shiver raced over her skin.

"Are you cold?" Apollyon slowed again, their pace becoming more leisurely.

"I'm fine," she whispered, taking in the sight of the Eiffel Tower and the world below.

"I should get you home."

"No." She grabbed his black and gold breastplate and he looked at her. She smiled shyly. "Just once around the tower?"

His smile was brilliant and her heart fluttered, her body responding to the feel of his hands on her again, growing aware of how close he was to her and the way he was looking at her with intense dark eyes that spoke of passion and need.

"Just one time." He soared lower, until they were barely metres above the ground when they passed over the river.

She looked down at her reflection but couldn't find one. They really were invisible. She laughed and none of the tourists snapping pictures of the tower noticed her.

They all ducked and grabbed at their clothes when Apollyon beat his wings again though and the wind they caused gusted through the crowds. The slight tilt to his lips as she glanced at him said he had enjoyed startling the tourists, and it was strange to discover he had a playful side. He had been so serious when she had met him, had been cold and distant in a way, but the more time she spent with him, the warmer he was becoming, opening up to her.

She was opening up to him too.

She knew it, and although she wanted to protect her heart, she was powerless to stop it from happening. Something about Apollyon had her unable to control herself, to shield herself from another possible heartbreak.

Serenity stared at the tower as they approached it, taking in a rare chance to see it so close but not from the inside. She would probably never see it like this again. It was incredible to think that Apollyon could do this all he wanted. He could fly around it until he got bored and then he could fly off somewhere else.

Apollyon held her close as they spiralled upwards, towards the bright top of the tower, and she gasped when he landed on the spike, one foot holding both of their weight and not affecting the tower at all.

"It's beautiful up here." She nestled in his arms to keep warm. She didn't want him to leave because she was cold. She wanted to stay here a while with him.

Pretending.

He wrapped his wings around her. The black feathers were warm against her arms and legs, covering her completely and shutting out the chill breeze.

Serenity looked up and found him staring at her, his head tilted to one side and his eyes full of warmth.

What was he thinking?

He had looked like that when she had thought he was going to kiss her.

Did he want to kiss her now?

She wanted it more than anything and it couldn't be just an act now because Edward wasn't around to see them.

It couldn't be an act.

His eyes dropped to her mouth.

Serenity forced herself to look at the city, away from Apollyon. She didn't want to get hurt again by getting her hopes up about him. Rebounding wasn't her style, and something told her that if she gave in to the desires burning inside her, she wouldn't be rebounding anyway. What she felt for Apollyon was terrifyingly real, and she couldn't risk getting her heart broken by him. She wasn't sure she would come back from that.

"You are getting cold," he said and she heard a different meaning to those words.

They cut her so deep that she felt as though she was bleeding inside. She wanted to tell him that she didn't mean to be distant and that she wanted him, but she couldn't find her voice.

He unfurled his wings, tilted forwards as he pushed off from the tower, and rocketed towards the ground so fast that she clung to his neck, afraid that he was going to drop her after all. He pulled up at the last second with a mighty beat of his wings and then they were soaring over the rooftops again, heading towards her home.

A jumble of words fought at the tip of her tongue but she held it because she could feel the change in his mood, could sense the way it had darkened through the power that constantly flowed from him and over her.

She didn't want to push him further, hadn't meant to ruin things, but it seemed to be what she always did.

Even when she didn't want to.

The silence pressed down on her, the hard set of Apollyon's jaw and the coldness of his blue eyes whenever she risked a glance at him weighing heavily on her heart. If she apologised, would it fix everything? Would he go back to smiling at her, laughing with her?

Serenity directed him once they were close, her heart heavy and her head aching. She wasn't sure what she was doing.

Was she imagining it all and just seeing what she wanted to see? Did she really feel something for Apollyon other than lust?

She had never been the sort to flirt with a man or look for a quick fling.

Was she serious about him?

# CHAPTER 7

Apollyon landed on the roof balcony of her apartment, touching down so gently that Serenity didn't even feel it, and his wings folded against his back. He set her down and she stood looking up at him, trying to figure out her feelings and what she was doing.

She barely knew him.

Yet the ocean of space that had opened between them cut at her, had her feeling as if she was bleeding inside as she waited for him to say something. Anything.

He remained cold and distant, staring down at her without a shred of emotion in his blue eyes.

It was probably best this way.

He was an angel.

She couldn't do this, she couldn't do it to herself. She had been hurting before Apollyon had come to her, but that pain would be nothing compared with the agony she would feel if she let this go on and got caught up in it all, believing it could be something.

She needed to protect herself, had to avert the disaster and the heartache she could plainly see looming ahead of her, and as much as it hurt to push him away, she would bear it to avoid that pain.

She would get her books back somehow, without Apollyon's help.

"Thank you." She straightened out her black dress, fidgeting with the hem.

"For flying you home?" He canted his head again.

"No... for helping me. It was very kind of you." Could she have sounded more stilted?

She wasn't sure how to act around him now. She waged war with herself as she looked at him, the thought of him leaving tearing at her and the need to throw herself into his arms to seize the moment and him raging through her.

Apollyon finally smiled and the coldness in his eyes melted away. "We have not had your vengeance yet."

She couldn't help but notice how focused he was on that aspect of her deal with him.

Edward had been jealous. That was all she needed, but it wasn't enough for Apollyon.

Just how far was he willing to go in order to make Edward suffer?

The hint of darkness in Apollyon's eyes warned he hadn't been lying to her and that he would do terrible things to Edward if she commanded it.

It was all getting out of control.

Someone was going to end up hurt if she let things continue and she had the awful feeling it was going to be her.

She opened her mouth to tell him that it was over and she would get her books back herself, and he didn't need to worry.

"Is it really okay for you to be doing this?" she said instead.

His smile widened, handsome and charming, devastating in its effect.

Her heart beat faster, racing at the thoughts that crowded her mind, a continuation of the way they had been dancing together. She had never been so bold with Edward when they had danced. Pretending it was all a charade had made her feel free and she had thrown herself into it, using making Edward jealous as an excuse to do as she wanted with Apollyon.

She wanted to dance like that with him again, right now on the rooftop under the moon.

"I can do as I please. Angels are not God's to command. We merely work for him, and a number work for the Devil."

"But you're definitely a good guy?" she whispered, not quite sure.

The things he had told her about his duty left her feeling as though there was a very wicked streak in him. Why else would they have chosen him to rain destruction down on Earth?

"I am." He stepped towards her, his tall broad build making her feel small. "You have that look again, the one that makes me feel as though you are about to say I am death."

"You're not." She sounded confident even when she wasn't. It surprised her. She stepped closer to him, tilting her head back to see into his eyes. Her heart hammered. "You're just a bad boy."

He grinned. "So I have been told."

She frowned. "By women?"

He shook his head, his expression gaining an amused edge. "No, by my fellow warriors. That was a long time ago, and we have not seen each other in many centuries."

"What happened?" Serenity studied his face, trying to read his feelings on it.

He didn't seem sad that he hadn't spoken to his friends in all that time, but his expression was guarded now, his eyes lacking emotion.

"Some remained constant, serving Heaven, and I have been assigned… elsewhere. Some of them changed." He walked to the edge of the small balcony set into the sloping grey roof and stared off into the distance. The breeze caught the strands of his dark ponytail and ruffled his feathers. He sighed and looked over his shoulder at her. "They chose to pass their years on Earth, in the arms of the mortal women they loved. We have a habit of watching humans, and celibacy in modern times is very difficult. Females dress so provocatively."

His gaze fell to her dress, slowly running over it from her breasts to her thighs. She kept still, feeling awkward from the heat in his eyes but not wanting them to leave her. She liked the feel of them on her and how confident his hungry looks made her.

That confidence shattered the hold her fear had on her, had her wanting to forget pushing him away and boldly pull him closer instead.

"They're allowed to do that?" she whispered, not quite able to find her voice, and his blue eyes jumped to hers.

She walked over to him, intending to close the distance just as she desired and see what he would do. Her nerve faltered and she ended up leaning her bottom against the black metal railing beside him instead. His gaze seared the side of her face, so intense that she could feel it and was powerless to stop herself from looking up into his eyes.

He laughed again but it didn't quell the fire in his eyes. It burned brighter now, flames that threatened to set her on fire too if she took the leap into his arms.

"We are angels." He cleared her fair hair from her face, tucking it back into her chignon. "Not saints."

"Oh." Her wide eyes fell and caught on his mouth.

How good would it feel to kiss him, to have his lips playing over her flesh, teasing her until she shattered and he had to put her back together again?

She shouldn't be wondering that, but she couldn't help herself, was losing the fight against the desire he stirred in her.

"Some fall and choose to become mortal... others remain as they are but serve from Earth. It is a great sacrifice on both accounts." He stroked her cheek, held her gaze for long seconds, and then stepped away from her, severing contact. "Today has been a lot for you to take in. I will let you rest and return tomorrow."

Serenity caught his wrist before he could move away. He looked down at her hand on him and then into her eyes.

She swallowed.

"Where will you go?" She released him and looked out across the rooftops as she picked at the paint on the railings, struggling to tamp down the sudden surge of nerves. She glanced at him. "Do you have friends here?"

"No." He moved closer to her again, until he was almost touching her and she could feel his power radiating against hers.

He was strong. His power was far more potent than hers was and she didn't doubt that he could be a deadly destructive force if he put his mind to it, but for some reason that didn't scare her. He hadn't given her a reason to fear him, only to trust him and feel safe around him, and the closer he was to her, the more she felt that way.

Serenity turned and plastered a smile on her face to cover her nerves. "You can stay here."

A single dark eyebrow rose at the suggestion.

"I have a couch you could sleep on, and some blankets, and it's better than being alone, right?"

His gaze raked over her again, giving her the impression that he was thinking of sleeping somewhere other than the couch, and then the passion that had been surfacing in his eyes melted away to reveal a feeling that surprised her. It looked a lot like relief or perhaps loneliness.

She reached out without thinking and touched his forearm, placing her hand on the black leather cuff that protected it, and tried to pinpoint the emotion using her power.

Apollyon frowned and took her hand. The sudden skin-on-skin contact boosted her senses and the feeling came through loud and clear. She stared at him as he toyed with her fingers, his attention fixed on them.

*Loneliness.*

"The couch sounds good." He lowered her hand. "I have not slept in a long time."

"You don't sleep?" She lifted the latch on the French windows of her balcony and walked into the dark room.

When she bumped into the old wooden kitchen table, she snapped her fingers and the lights came on. She looked back at Apollyon where he stood near the door, his gaze scanning her kitchen and dining room.

It wasn't much.

The white walls needed a new coat to make them vibrant again and there was a stack of washing in the sink of the compact kitchen to her left and a pile of laundry on the table. She wasn't exactly painting herself in the best light by letting him see her home.

"Not when I am on duty, unless I am given leave to." Apollyon stepped forwards into the dining room and Serenity mulled over what he had said as she crossed the room to the open wooden door and went through into the living room. "I only sleep when on Earth. It has been centuries since I was last here."

"And I called you." She hadn't forgotten that. He had been surprised, and so had she. She snapped her fingers again, using her power to turn on the lamp in the corner of the living room behind the television. She pointed to the cream couch, hoping he wouldn't comment on the haphazard stacks of old books that littered the coffee table and the floor near it. "I'll get some blankets."

Serenity felt his gaze on her as she walked away, into her bedroom. The door was to the right of the television, directly in front of the couch. If she left it open, she would be able to see him while he slept. She grabbed one of the pillows from her double bed and then took a thick dark red blanket from the bottom of her wooden wardrobe to the right of the door.

Apollyon was sitting on the couch leafing through one of the books when she walked back out. He lifted his blue gaze from the pages and smiled when she held out the blanket.

"You have many books." He flicked to the next page, scanned it and raised his eyes to her again. "Are the ones Edward took like these?"

She shook her head. "No. They're far more valuable to my coven. These are mine."

He turned to the next page and her eyes widened as she spotted her hand-writing all over it. She lunged for it but he held it away from her and frowned at the page.

"You write in your books?" He arched an eyebrow at that, as if it was a crime.

Serenity grabbed it but he refused to let go. "It's easier than writing on paper and forgetting where I put it. It's only pencil, and I was making adjustments to the spell."

She cringed as she said that and his eyes drifted back to the page and slowly widened. She should have kept her mouth shut.

"Love spells?" He turned the book so he could read the spine and then looked up at her. "Why would you need to adjust a love spell?"

He looked genuinely interested in the answer, and a dash curious too.

"I needed it more potent for a client. Have you met many witches?" Maybe she was his first.

"I have met one before." His expression sobered. "She was under the protection of a friend, and fell under my protection too since he had been part of my team."

Serenity caught the glimmer of remorse as it flitted across his eyes, and the touch of sorrow that laced it, and held her tongue. Whoever the angel had been, and whoever the witch had been, Apollyon had lost them.

She took the book from him and carefully closed it, giving him time to come out of his thoughts.

When he finally looked at her, she smiled softly.

"I tend to wake early. I'll try to be quiet if you're sleeping." She set the book down on the low coffee table in front of the couch and lingered, part of her not wanting to leave him yet.

"Thank you." Apollyon nodded. "Goodnight, Serenity."

She smiled at the sound of her name on his tongue, spoken with warmth.

"Goodnight, Apollyon."

He smiled back at her.

Serenity took herself into her room and shut the door, pressing her back to it and closing her eyes.

How was she supposed to sleep with him in the next room?

It was going to be impossible.

# CHAPTER 8

Serenity opened the bedroom door a crack and peered through. The lights in the living room were off but the moon had moved around, shining through the windows to her right beyond the television.

She slowly swept her eyes over to Apollyon.

They widened.

His wings were gone.

She opened the door, convinced that she was dreaming it, and took a good look at him.

They were gone. He hadn't tucked them away. They just weren't there.

He lay on the couch, his head at the end nearest the door to the kitchen, and his feet dangling over the end beside the windows. She stifled her giggle at the sight of him sprawled out so uncomfortably. He was far too tall for her small couch. She probably should have given him the bed and slept on the couch herself.

Serenity snuck into the room, tiptoeing and grimacing with each step in case it made a noise. She wanted to look at him for a while and she didn't want to wake him. If he thought her black dress had been provocative, she could well imagine what he would think of the small dark red slip she was wearing.

She stopped a few feet from him, on the other side of the coffee table. He was beautiful bathed in moonlight and looked so normal without his wings. She could easily fool herself into thinking he was mortal just like her.

His bare chest slowly rose and fell, the pace of his breathing measured and deep. Her mouth turned dry when she looked him over.

He was naked.

Clearly, he wasn't used to sharing with female company.

The red blanket rode low, barely covering his hips, in danger of falling off completely. Her eyes wandered over him, soaking up every detail, every dip and swell of his delicious torso. He had one arm tucked behind his head and the other rested on his hip, drawing her gaze back there. It traced the curve of muscle that arched over his hip and then the dark line of hair that led her eyes downwards.

Looking at him now, it was hard to believe that he was a real angel.

Yet she was a witch.

Her mother had taught her to believe in everything, because you never knew what might just turn out to be real. She had always believed in angels but had never thought she would end up with one sleeping naked on her couch.

It just seemed so incredible to look at him and know that it was possible that he had lived for an eternity already.

He was immortal.

A very handsome immortal.

His face was a mask of peace as he slumbered and his dark hair was falling out of his ponytail and spread over his forearm where it disappeared under his head.

Were all angels as beautiful as Apollyon?

Her eyes drifted over him again, from the chiselled perfection of his face, to his broad shoulders, over the flat slabs of his pectorals and his dark nipples, to the tempting ridges of his abdomen.

He twitched and loosed a quiet moan.

Serenity stiffened, her heart leaping into her throat.

When he moved again, she bolted into her bedroom and dived under the covers, hiding there and pretending to be asleep. Her pulse thundered, blood rushing through her head, and she struggled to hear over it as she listened hard for a sign that she had woken him.

When only silence reached her ears, she breathed a sigh of relief and relaxed into the mattress.

The light burst on.

Serenity shot up in bed, clutching the dark pink covers to her chest, and her eyes flew wide.

She slapped her hands over them, her cheeks blazing over what she had just seen. "Cover yourself!"

Prickly heat chased over her skin at the flash of him stood naked in her doorway.

"You seemed rather interested in seeing it a moment ago." There was a hint of amusement in his voice.

Her whole body burned with her blush. "I am not... was not."

"You can come out now," he said.

She peeked through her fingers to make sure he wasn't tricking her.

It was cruel of him to stand before her like that when she wanted him. He had said that other angels had mortal women, but she still couldn't get past the fact that he was an angel and what she had been brought up to believe. Angels didn't do that sort of thing. They were good. They were saints.

Apollyon was bad. Apollyon was built for sin.

She knew it in her heart whenever she looked at him. He exuded power and sensuality, a lithe beautiful creature with the body of a god and the smile of a devil. She wanted him and if he hadn't put himself away then she was likely to reach out and take for once in her life.

Serenity's gaze slowly lowered to his hips. His small black loincloth covered him.

She emerged from her hiding place.

"Better?" He crossed the room and sat down beside her on the bed, one leg up on the mattress so he was almost facing her and the wall. "Were you having trouble sleeping?"

Was she ever? Did he know how impossible it was to resist him? To sit here in a big bed alone while he slept just a few metres away, nude?

Their dance still had her fired up.

"A little." She brought her knees up under the covers. "I don't know what I'm doing. Revenge really isn't my style."

"Let it be my revenge then."

Serenity looked at him and frowned. "Why?"

Apollyon sighed, leaned closer and feathered his fingers across her cheek and then sifted them through the long wild strands of her hair, wreaking havoc on her control.

"Because I saw your pain and felt your suffering, even before we met, and I want him to feel that too. I want to repay him for hurting you so deeply."

He really had been watching her. Her own guardian angel. He had seen her pain and then he had heard her call, and he had come to her, to ease her suffering and make her feel better.

Serenity didn't know what to say. It touched her that he clearly cared about her, enough that he would take the burden of revenge on his shoulders, lifting the weight from hers. It would still feel as though this was her revenge, even though he had said it was his, but she was thankful to have his support and to hear him say that he was in this with her.

"Thank you." She leaned over and pressed a kiss to his cheek.

She hesitated there, her mouth close to his and her heart beating wildly, awaiting his reaction. She hadn't thought about what she was doing. It had been instinct to kiss him.

He was still a moment, as though she had shocked him, and then he turned.

Claimed her lips in a kiss that seared her.

She instantly melted into it, swept up in the passionate play of his mouth over hers, and couldn't hold back a moan as his tongue slipped between her lips to tease her. She tilted her head and leaned into the kiss, aching for more, bewitched by the hard demanding feel of it.

His mouth was warm, inviting, and she didn't pause to think. She focused on feeling instead, because everything about it felt right to her. She skimmed her hands over his shoulders as his claimed her waist, and she moaned as ripples of pleasure ran through her, sending her desire soaring.

His tongue delved into her mouth again, stealing her breath away, and he moved on the bed, kneeling and leaning into her, driving her into submission.

She went willingly, relaxing back into the pillows, eager for more, for whatever he would give to her.

His bare chest pressed against hers, the hard feel of him divine and delicious, and she couldn't resist gripping his biceps. They flexed beneath her fingers as he kissed her, drawing another moan from her lips. He was strong. Powerful. Everything about him spoke to her most feminine side, had her wild with a need to take things further than just kissing.

He groaned, a low guttural sound that sent a tremble through her, and her eyes slipped shut.

When he broke for air and lingered looking at her for a moment, sense reared its ugly head and she considered what she was doing.

She was kissing an angel.

"Wait." She pressed her hands against his chest, heat flooding her at the silk on steel feel of it beneath her palms that threatened to shatter her control again.

"No," he breathed and kissed her again, sweeping his tongue across her lips and teasing her, tempting her into surrendering. "I do not want to stop."

Serenity caved for a moment, melting under the feel of his hands gliding up her sides, lifting her satin slip with them, heading towards her breasts. Reality kicked in again when they neared her chest and she pushed harder against his.

"Stop."

Apollyon pulled back, leaning over her, his warm breath washing her face.

"Is something wrong?" His blue eyes questioned hers.

"What are you doing?"

He frowned. "Exactly what I want to do for once."

He dipped his head to kiss her again and she almost relented. Almost. She braced her hands against his chest and leaned back so he couldn't reach her.

"You want this," he whispered and stroked her sides, getting closer to her breasts.

She shivered, tiny jolts of bliss skittering across her skin. He was right, she did want it, but she just couldn't get past the fact that he was an angel.

"Won't you get into trouble?" She searched his eyes. "I don't want to get you into trouble."

He smiled and her resistance melted a little. "I won't. You drive me crazy. I need you, Serenity. Being close to you tonight, seeing you laughing, smiling, happy because of me... I want to make you feel that way again, and I know you want it too. Somewhere along the line tonight, it stopped being an act for me. It became real."

He smoothed her hair across the dark pink pillow, his eyes warm and honest, backing up his words. He wasn't lying. She hadn't been alone tonight. The desire he had shown to her hadn't been pretend.

He wanted her.

Relief poured through her, washing away the last of her doubts, unleashing the need she kept trying to bottle up and deny.

"Is it the same for you?" He looked hopeful and she sensed his nerves, his need to know he wasn't alone.

Serenity didn't hesitate.

She nodded. "It is... I just... with the wings gone it's so much easier to fool myself, but I know that you're an angel... it—"

Apollyon pressed a lone finger to her lips. "Forget everything everyone ever told you about us. We can be with mortals and we are free to do as we please. Besides, you are my master right now. Whatever you want of me, you will have, but resisting you is becoming impossible."

She felt the same way. She had tried her hardest but she didn't want to resist him now. She wanted to give herself to him, ached to fulfil the deep craving to have his body on hers, to drown in his kisses and lose herself in the moment.

Apollyon *had* made her happy tonight.

She had felt as though Edward had never happened and that being in Apollyon's arms was enough to bring a smile back to her face. He had made her laugh for the first time in weeks.

But none of that erased the fear in her heart that he was going to disappear when he'd had his vengeance and she would be alone again.

She shut out the voices that warned her against going through with it and ran her hands over Apollyon's strong shoulders, caressing his bronzed skin and feeling his warmth.

"Where did the wings go?" She focused on touching him, using it to push out the doubts and slowly loosen the tethers of her control.

She wanted him.

She could do this.

"Away." He looked at her left hand where it stroked his right shoulder and then back into her eyes. "I can keep them like this if I concentrate, but it only works for a short time. It was uncomfortable to sleep on them. Would you like me to bring them back?"

"Not right now." Serenity ran her hands up his neck to his jaw and stroked the square line of it, her gaze drifting over his face and putting it to memory. She would never forget it, and she wasn't likely to find a man as handsome as him again. "Right now, I like you just the way you are."

"Naked?" he said and she couldn't help smiling at his innocent expression.

"Naked," she whispered, not needing to look to know that what little he had been wearing was now gone.

She slid one her hand around the nape of his neck and drew him down to her. With a wicked smile, she showed him he wasn't the only one who could perform magic and made her satin slip disappear, leaving her naked beneath the dark covers.

Apollyon groaned, his gaze running over her chest with blatant desire even though her nipples were still hidden. What would he look like when she was naked before him? She couldn't wait to find out.

She pressed her lips to his and he immediately tilted his head and fused their mouths in another hungry kiss. She let go this time, not thinking about tomorrow, only thinking about now and how good it felt to be in Apollyon's arms.

She wouldn't give this up for anything.

If he was brave enough to take what he wanted, then she would too. She would live with the consequences and pay whatever price she had to in order to have this moment with him.

His tongue brushed hers and she moaned and clutched his shoulder, drawing him closer until his chest was covering hers again, his hands caressing her upper arms. On a low groan, he broke away from her mouth and pressed long kisses down her jaw and her neck, sending shivers chasing over her skin, spreading outwards from where his lips touched.

She reached up above her head, clutched the pillow and closed her eyes as he feathered his lips over her collarbone and then down her chest. Her breath left her in a sigh and she arched into his touch, aching for more as he teased her, had her restless with a need for him to kiss her breasts.

"You taste good," Apollyon murmured against her skin and she looked at him, meeting his gaze.

He drew the dark covers down, revealing the swell of her breasts, sending anticipation swirling through her. His eyes left hers, dropping to her chest, and his moan was purely masculine. Her own moan joined it as he lowered his head and she arched up to meet him, unable to hold back and stop herself.

The first brush of his lips over her pebbled nipple sent sparks shooting outwards from its centre and rekindled the embers of the fire he had lit in her when they had danced. She moaned again, sank her teeth into her lower lip and tugged on it as he stroked his tongue over her nipple. Heat pooled lower, gathering in her belly as she watched him, couldn't tear her eyes away from him as he slowly worshipped her breast.

His thumb grazed the underside of her other one and his fingers curled around to cup it, the heat of his palm against her almost too much to bear.

He moved across to it, swirling his tongue around the dusky peak and sending another shower of sparks across her skin. "So good."

Serenity arched against him, pressing her nipple into his mouth, and he groaned and sucked it. Her groin throbbed, hot with need, aching to have his attention as he thumbed her other nipple, teasing it so it remained aroused and making her burn for him.

She wanted to touch him too, to kiss him and taste his skin. She wanted to lick every inch of him until he moaned her name and begged for more, until he was as wild and lost as he was making her.

She ran her hands up his biceps, delighting in tracing the lines of his strong muscles. Just the sight of him had made her hot and bothered, but the feel of him took her beyond that, filling her with a desperate urge to push him onto his back and make love to him.

Not quite make love.

What was going around her head at ten positions a second was definitely raw and animalistic, a hard coupling that would leave her knees weak and make every part of her tremble.

She moaned at the thought and the feel of Apollyon at her breasts, taking her out of her mind with his constant torture of her nipples. Her breasts were tight, aching from the feel of his attention, and she raked her nails down his arms when he sucked harder and thrust her chest up. He slid a hand beneath her and held her to him, groaning, his pleasure flowing through her, into her and cranking her tighter.

She wanted more.

Needed more.

Serenity pushed at the covers, needing to feel his hot body against the whole of hers, wanting his delicious weight on her.

Wanting to be at his mercy.

Apollyon stepped off the bed and her gaze was immediately on him, shamelessly drinking her fill of his body. He whipped the covers off her and stood there, long hard cock twitching and jerking as his hungry dark gaze roamed over her bare curves.

Serenity rubbed her thighs together, drawing his attention there, wanting to feel it on her and wanting to see the passion in his eyes when he looked. There was so much desire in his expression, so much heat and need as he stared at her.

It made her feel powerful, sexy, and brave.

Apollyon groaned when she ran her hands over her breasts, teasing her own nipples, and then the black slashes of his eyebrows knitted hard when she skimmed her fingers down her sides and dipped them in at the apex of her thighs, brushing them across her mound.

"Devil," he whispered and walked around the bed, his gaze never leaving her.

His chest heaved, muscles straining and taut, keeping her hungry eyes locked on him. He looked incredible as he prowled, his focus fixed on her hands. She didn't stop. Each time she swept her fingers over the triangle of fair hair at the apex of her thighs, he moaned and his cock bobbed.

Serenity licked her lips. She wanted to taste that too. She wanted to wrap her lips around every hard inch of him, take him deep into her mouth, and suck him until he was crying her name to the heavens and clutching her to him.

She wanted it and she was going to do it.

She rolled onto her knees, coming to face him.

Apollyon frowned as she crawled towards him where he stood at the foot of the bed.

She kneeled before him and held his dark gaze as she lightly wrapped her fingers around his hard length. His eyelids slipped to half-mast when she moved her hand down, exposing the crown of his cock, and he shuddered.

"How long has it been since you've had a woman?" she whispered up at him, intent on getting answers while he was at her mercy.

She wanted to hear him say it again, to know that he was telling the truth.

"Too long," he muttered and opened his eyes and looked at her when she didn't continue. "Many centuries. I would not lie to you, Serenity. I have been in Hell for millennia and the only woman I have truly looked at in that time is you."

Her heart gave a hard beat against her chest.

Right answer.

Serenity returned her gaze to his hard length and ran her hand down it again, drawing another breathy moan from Apollyon.

She leaned forwards and he gasped when she licked the head, swirling her tongue around the blunt crown and tasting him.

His hands leaped to her shoulders, his grip tight and bordering on painful.

She didn't stop.

She tasted him again, stroking her tongue up the seam and brushing her lips over it. Heat pooled at the apex of her thighs at the thought of him inside her, taking her, being with her. She wanted that. It was torture to wait but she would. She wanted to know him all over and then she wanted him to know her from the inside.

Apollyon groaned again when she wrapped her mouth around his cock and sucked him, teasing only the head at first and then taking him deeper. He tangled one hand in her hair as his breath stuttered, his thighs tensing and pressing his length deeper still. She moaned and held him tightly with her right hand and flicked her tongue over the sensitive head, eliciting another deep rumbling groan from him.

The tight feeling inside her increased with each moan that left his lips, the feeling of power increasing with them too and making her hunger rise. She sucked him harder, holding him still with her hand so he couldn't thrust. He tried, desperate short movements accompanied by wicked sounding moans when he found he was at her mercy.

She was in control now.

Or so she thought.

Before she could figure out what was happening, he was gone from her hand and her mouth and she was on her back on the bed.

She gasped when he buried his face between her thighs and licked the length of her, sending a shockwave of sensation ripping through her.

He didn't give her a chance to catch her breath. He grabbed her ankles, hooking them over his broad shoulders, and raised her bottom off the bed, so only her shoulders and head were touching it as he went to war on her.

Serenity moaned and writhed under the heated caress of his tongue, clutched the sheets into her tight fists as she silently begged him for more. She wanted release. She wanted to explode into a thousand tiny pieces in his arms and under the blissful ministrations of his tongue.

He flicked her sensitive bead with it, sending prickly hot tingles sweeping over her belly and thighs, and clamped his hands over her thighs, anchoring her to him.

She wriggled, rubbing against his face, desperate for the one flick of his tongue that would send her over the edge.

She was so close.

Apollyon released her before it happened, lowering her legs from his shoulders and breathing hard. She panted along with him, trying to gather her scattered senses, and piecing herself back together so she could chastise him for stopping.

Her eyes opened and she met his dark hungry gaze, shivered under the intensity of it that stole her voice. Heat followed his eyes as he ran them over her body, lingering on her breasts and thighs, and she squirmed again, aching for him to touch her, to kiss and lick her.

To give her the release she needed.

He grabbed her hips and she gasped as he dragged her to the edge of the bed and his hard hot length pressed against her core. A groan fell from her lips as her mind filled with the thought of him thrusting into her and she couldn't stop herself from rubbing against it.

He pressed her hips into the bed, stopping her, and her gaze met his again.

The passion in his eyes, the raw need, spoke to her.

It made her feel alive, made her burn hotter still.

She freed her legs from beside his hips and ran her feet over the pronounced muscles of his stomach to his pectorals. He lightly caught her ankle and kissed it, his eyes never leaving hers, and she quivered and moaned as he took hold of her other one, bringing it to rest on his shoulder.

Serenity waited, her eyes on his, her body calling him.

She sighed when he ran the head of his cock over her, teasing her pert bead with it, driving her to the edge again, and then closed her eyes and moaned as he slowly filled her. Inch after inch. She trembled at the feel of him stretching her, going deep into her body, until his balls brushed her backside. It was divine.

Her legs slipped, catching on his arms and resting there with her knees at his elbows.

He grasped her hips and she opened her eyes again, intent on seeing his as he took her, needing to know the pleasure he felt as he joined them was as intense and overwhelming as the bliss that was flooding her.

Another sighing moan escaped her when he eased his length almost fully out and his groan joined it when he slid back in, deep and slow, until his pelvic bone brushed her pert bundle of nerves.

He withdrew again, quicker this time, and thrust back in, gradually building the pace until it was hard to keep her focus on him and not close her eyes. She placed her hands over his and held them as he groaned and thrust harder, until his whole body tensed and his grip on her thighs began to hurt.

She didn't care.

She wanted to feel his power, needed to feel him inside her. He pumped hard and deep as if he knew that need, slamming against her sensitive bead each time their hips met, sending her breasts wobbling. She tensed around his cock, groaning with him, low and deep, desperate in her search for release.

It came in a blinding flash, sending a wave of scorching heat over her body and she moaned as her thighs tingled and quivered, shaking against him. He didn't stop. He drove harder, longer strokes that built the fire inside her again, until she was clutching his hands, uttering quiet pleas for more.

Apollyon groaned each time he entered her, filling the bedroom with the deliciously guttural and animalistic sound as he thrust faster and faster, until she was on the verge of crumbling into pieces again.

Serenity arched her back, choking him in her warm depths, and drawing a deep hard thrust from him as a response. She did it again, teasing him, trying to draw him to the edge with her. He raised her bottom from the bed and tore a moan from her throat instead when he plunged deeper, taking all of her.

He gave a groan that she could only think of as a low growl and slammed into her core, his cock throbbing and spilling his warm seed. She clenched her muscles around him, aching to climax too.

His hand delved between them and she groaned when the feel of him pulsing and the sweep of his thumb over her nub sent stars spinning across her eyes and heat sweeping through her. Her body kicked and throbbed, trembling as fiercely as his as he held her in place, moaning quietly as her muscles squeezed his softening cock.

When she could breathe again, she lazily ran her eyes over his body, slowly taking in every inch of him. A fine sheen of sweat covered him now, his bronzed skin shining with it and radiating power and beauty.

It took her a moment to find the courage to look him in the eye. When she did, she found him smiling at her, his eyes a vivid shade of blue now as though his climax had affected them.

He held her still, remaining inside her, with her legs hooked over his arms.

His cock twitched and her eyes widened when he raked his gaze over her body and she felt him growing hard again.

He gave her a wicked smile and pulled out of her, only to lean over her and suck her right nipple into his mouth.

Serenity stared at the ceiling, lost in the hazy warmth of two orgasms and feeling as though she was shortly going to add a third.

And maybe a fourth.

And he said she was a devil.

# CHAPTER 9

Apollyon smiled ear to ear as he stretched out in the bed, causing the dark pink covers to ride low on his hips. He couldn't recall a time he had felt so relaxed. So content.

So at home.

Serenity slept beside him, curled up on her side with her hands around his right arm and her cheek pressed against his biceps. Her soft, slow breathing filled his ears, adding to the sensation of warmth and peace flowing through him.

He stroked the rogue strands of blonde hair from her face so he could see it better and stilled as his fingers brushed her fair skin and her feelings flowed into him, strengthening his own as hers echoed them. He wasn't the only one who had enjoyed last night.

When she had started showing signs of tiredness, he had stopped and contented himself with watching her sleep instead, enjoying the smile that had remained on her lips long after she had started dreaming. She was beautiful when she slept, beautiful when she was awake, beautiful when she screamed his name during her climax.

She had done that a few times.

Any immortal within at least two miles and any mortal in her building would have heard her. His smile stretched a little wider as pride ran through him again, born of the fact he had managed to make her shriek at the top of her lungs.

She had blushed violently afterwards and then burst into giggles that had given him pause, had made him go still so he could absorb her reaction. He loved the way she laughed. He loved that it had been because of him.

After watching her from afar for so long, seeing her suffering, it felt good to be able to do something to alleviate her sorrow and chase the clouds from her heart.

Sunlight cast a warm glow through the white muslin curtains, shafts of it cutting through the room to streak across him and Serenity.

It was growing late.

He stifled a yawn that crept up on him and blinked away sleep as it finally tried to claim him. He hadn't slept much during the night. Serenity had fascinated him too much and he had lost himself in watching her.

It had been dawn before he had realised it and he had dozed for a while, resting in her arms, but had woken from time to time to check Serenity was still beside him, tucked close to him as she slumbered.

He had never slept with someone like that before—held close by them, feeling protected in their embrace and content.

It was strange, but wonderful.

Apollyon rolled onto his side, watching over his angel as she slept.

He wanted to wake her, to have her look at him and see her smile, but she needed to rest. She had been through so much recently and he had seen how it had affected her. Her smile had disappeared but he had brought it back and it felt as though he had made the sun shine again.

Apollyon pressed a light kiss to her forehead and gently removed her hands from his arm. She murmured a quiet protest, wrinkled her nose, and burrowed into her pillow instead. He rolled out of the bed and pulled the covers up to her shoulders, and stood there a moment, looking down at her as sunlight cast a warm glow over her, making her fair hair shine.

Beautiful.

He could look at her forever.

On a deep sigh, he forced himself to turn away. He waved his hand over himself, putting his black loincloth back in place, and padded quietly from the bedroom and through the living room to the kitchen.

It was darker in the small kitchen and dining room, the sun not reaching them from the rest of the apartment. It hit a small area of the patio ahead of him though, and he found himself drawn to it.

His shoulders itched and he rolled them, trying to ease the tension building there.

His wings wanted out.

He hadn't confined them for this long in millennia. He hadn't needed to. Sleeping on them had been painful though, so despite the fact it consumed a lot of energy and took a lot of effort to get them to disappear, he had forced them away.

And he had kept them away because Serenity seemed to like him without wings. It certainly made whatever reservations she had about him disappear anyway.

She thought angels were saints.

He had definitely disproven that theory last night.

He smiled, lifted the latch on the French doors, and walked out onto the balcony.

The high sun shone down on his bare back when he reached the black railings around the balcony, warming his skin until his tension melted away. He sighed and unfurled his wings, spreading them out so they stretched the width of the patio and extended over the sloping roof on either side of it.

He flapped them, aligning his black feathers, and curled his right wing towards him so he could preen it. It felt good to release them for a while and feel the sunshine on them.

He would put them away again before Serenity woke. Now that he was making progress with her, he didn't want to scare her off. He wasn't sure whether the sight of his wings would do that but he didn't want to risk it.

Did his fellow warriors who had left their position to be with a female have this problem?

He wished there was one nearby so he could speak to them about it.

Apollyon stared out over the grey roofs of the Paris suburb as he pondered what he was going to do next, where this mission of vengeance was taking him. His gaze drifted over the leafy avenue below and his ears filled with the quiet sound of cars passing in the distance.

His fellow warriors probably hadn't fallen for a witch.

A smile tugged at his lips again. A witch. She worried what people would make of him if they could see his black wings. What would they make of her if they knew that she possessed powers that were only real in most humans' imaginations?

"Mmm, there you are." Her voice was hushed, lazy and full of happiness that he could feel in her as she stepped out onto the balcony behind him. "I thought I had lost you."

His eyes slipped shut when she ran her hands up his back and stroked the start of his wings, her palms gliding between them along his spine. A groan rose in his throat as her fingers skimmed along the point where his wings connected to his shoulders and teased them.

Damn, that felt good.

Apollyon kept still, enjoying the feel of her hands running over his feathers and not wanting to scare her away. She giggled when he folded his wings, the sound light in the air, no trace of fear or any negative emotion in it.

She skimmed her hands across the breadth of his furled wings and then down the outside of them, teasing his flight feathers, her touch light and soothing.

"I wish I had wings," she whispered.

He slowly turned to face her. "You do?"

She nodded and cast a glance over them, from the point where they arched above his head to the tips of his longest feathers where they grazed his calves. "They're beautiful. If I had wings, I'd never stop flying."

"You are beginning to sound like an angel. We love nothing more than to fly." Another smile tugged at his lips as he caught the sparkle in her eyes, a shimmer of something that looked a little like envy.

"Really? Nothing more than flying?" Her lips curved into a smile and a hint of colour touched her cheeks. "Could have fooled me."

He grinned at her insinuation. He loved that too, but flying had a special place in his heart, as it did with all angels. Taking her up last night, standing atop the Eiffel Tower with her, had been magical and had made him realise just how deeply he had missed flying when he had been stuck in Hell. He hadn't wanted to leave, could have stayed there all night with her in his arms, tucked safely in his wings, but she had been cold and kissing her had become too tempting.

"Come inside and I'll find us some breakfast." She walked towards the doors.

His gaze fell to her body and he bit back a groan. Her small dark red slip hugged her curves, shifting in a sensual way with each step, threatening to get him going again. He couldn't take his eyes off her slender legs or her backside as it swayed. Divine.

He was staring at her so much that he forgot about his wings.

Pain ricocheted along the length of the bones as they banged against the doorframe and he grimaced and focused, trying to make them disappear.

"You could just duck like you did last night." Her gaze landed on him, had heat flaring in his veins but it was her words that stopped him dead and had him staring at her.

Was she approving of his wings now?

The thought that she might be and the affectionate shine in her hazel eyes brought a smile to his lips, one he couldn't contain and quickly became a grin as it dawned on him that his wings weren't the barrier between them he had feared they were.

He ducked and kept his wings tucked so he didn't knock anything over in the dining room.

Serenity walked into the small pale kitchen, opened a tall white box that he recognised as a refrigerator, and looked inside. He leaned to his left so he could see the contents, curious as to what it contained. There was milk and cheese, things he had often seen in the pool and could easily recognise, but there was other food he couldn't identify.

Studying the mortal world from a distance did have its drawbacks.

Most of the time, people didn't mention what things were called so he couldn't hear their names. Sometimes, he would receive briefing documents that kept him up to date with the latest inventions so he was prepared for being called to Earth, or other angels would tell him of things they had experienced if they had a reason to come down to the bottomless pit.

His stomach growled at the sight of the food.

He pressed a hand to it and frowned. He had forgotten how much energy he used when on Earth. Due to the circumstances of his eternal duty, he was one of only a few angels who didn't need to eat or sleep when they were in Hell as well as in Heaven. On Earth, things were different. Certain parts of him changed or switched off, and other parts switched on. Hunger was one of them.

Serenity bent over, revealing the curve of her bare bottom.

His body ached at the sight.

Lust seemed to be another.

But he was beginning to feel that this was something other than lust.

She took a pot from the refrigerator and pulled a black machine away from the back of the kitchen counter. He studied her movements, curious and unable to curb the desire to learn new things about the mortal world. She filled a large glass jug with water and poured it into the machine.

What was she doing?

"Do you want some coffee?" Her breezy smile turned shy and she muttered, "Maybe not."

She had figured out what effect coffee had on him then.

He hadn't exactly done the best job of concealing it, so he wasn't surprised that she had noticed.

He walked into the kitchen, until he was close enough to her that he could feel her heat and smell her sweet floral scent, and that ache in his body grew worse, pressing him to do something about it.

"I could go for a cup, if you are." He raked his gaze over her, memorising the subtle curves hidden beneath her red satin slip, recalling how good she had looked bared to him.

Her cheeks matched the colour of it when his eyes met hers again.

"Are you hungry?" She glanced away, at the cupboards, an awkward edge to her air.

"Starved." He pulled her against him and kissed her, swallowing her small gasp.

Her hands landed on his bare chest as he slid his over her hips, and for a moment, he thought she was going to stop him again, but then she moaned and kissed him, her lips dancing softly over his, stirring fire in his veins.

Apollyon pressed her against the kitchen counter and gathered her into his arms, his tongue tangling with hers and stealing her breathy moans. He savoured each one as he held her, lost himself in her all over again. The world fell away until there was only her. Only her hands as they wandered over his chest, warm against his skin, setting him aflame wherever she touched. Only her as she kissed him deeper, stoked his passion and hunger so it built inside him, twisting him tight with a need to have more of her.

To drown in her.

He groaned and angled his head so he could kiss her deeper still, could pour out the need that felt as if it might rip him apart if he didn't find a way to make it flow out of him.

She pulled back, breathing hard, and smiled shakily, her eyes dark with the need he could feel in her.

He stared at her mouth, hungry to kiss her again, finding it hard to give her a moment to catch her breath. She twirled under his arm and out of his reach, going back to the black machine and pressing a button.

"Do you want a shower?" She turned back to him.

"With you?" He could go along with that idea.

She blushed again. "I was thinking alone."

"I have been alone long enough." He smiled but it faltered and he frowned at the sudden feeling of emptiness inside him.

He had been happy a moment ago.

Before that, he had been content.

And before meeting her he had been fine.

No. He hadn't been fine.

He had been lonely.

Meeting her had made him realise that.

He had watched her so much that he had lost awareness of the feeling. It had drifted to the back of his mind, put there by how often he saw her in the pool. She had chased away his loneliness even back then, making him feel as though he wouldn't be waiting forever and he wasn't alone. He had known her, studied her, stalked her as she put it, and he had never realised.

Not until he had met her.

He had watched her in the pool, had watched her smile and laugh, each of them touching his heart without him knowing it, and had felt her pain when she had been sad and hurt. He had responded to it, desired to assist her and make her feel better so she would be happy again.

She had called.

He had responded because he had feelings for her.

Apollyon tensed when her fingers lightly brushed his cheek and shook himself back to her.

She stood before him, smiling up into his eyes. A smile for him. He had brought it back and now she smiled even when she was confused. Her feelings travelled through her touch and into him, deep into his heart where he could decipher them.

She was concerned and he knew what she was going to ask.

"Where did the serious look come from?" she whispered with a small frown, searching his eyes as though they held the answer.

He caught her hand, kissed her palm and smiled.

He had feelings for her. That was where his sudden seriousness had come from. That and the question ringing in his mind.

Could she love him?

Was it really possible for a mortal to love an angel?

# CHAPTER 10

Apollyon wished more than ever that some of his fellow warriors were in Paris as questions crowded his mind, weighing him down and leaving him uncertain of himself. He needed to ask them if it was truly possible for a mortal to love an angel so he could ease the strange tight sensation in his chest.

*Fear.*

It was cold and sharp, felt as if it was hollowing him out inside. It wasn't fear in the passing sort of way, like the fear he'd had about her not being able to see past his wings. This was genuine fear, bone-deep and crushing, suffocating him.

He shook it away but it was hard to let it go, even when he reminded himself that he had never felt fear, not even when he had faced the Devil and cast him into the bottomless pit for millennia. He wasn't going to start now. He wasn't going to be afraid of Serenity.

He would make her fall for him.

He would make her love him.

"It's nothing." He kissed her hand again and then her wrist, working his way up to her elbow. "What about that shower?"

"What about the coffee?"

Apollyon grinned, lifted her onto the kitchen counter, and settled himself between her thighs.

"I do not need the coffee." He rubbed himself against her, lost himself a little again as pleasure built inside him and he made a new discovery.

Kitchen counters were a good height, perfect in fact.

"I can see that." She ran her hands around his hips, sending a shiver over his skin that only added fuel to the fire blazing inside him. "We can shower later."

He liked the sound of that. Right now though, he was going to make love with her and make her see that this wasn't lust that he was feeling.

Serenity stroked his shoulders and touched his feathers again. He wasn't going to make them go away. She had to be his like this, while he looked like himself, not like a mortal. He didn't want to hide any part of him from her. He needed her to accept him as a whole.

Apollyon skimmed his hands up her thighs, slipping them under the hem of her red satin slip and raising it. He ached at the sight of the neat thatch of curls at the apex of her thighs and clutched her backside, bringing her right to the edge of the counter. She dragged her fingertips down his chest, over his stomach, and to his hips again.

They stopped there, running along the waist of his black loincloth, and he sensed her hesitation.

She didn't know how to undo it.

He went to remove it for her but she snapped her fingers and it was gone, and so was her slip.

Where did she send things when she did that?

He pushed his curiosity away and focused on the moment instead, filing a mental note to ask her about her powers later. A moan trembled on her lips as he cupped her breasts and she frowned at him as he stroked his palms down her body, tracing her curves.

She sighed when he feathered his fingers up her thighs and then delved between them, teasing her.

She teased him by leaning back, planting her hands against the counter behind her to support herself, and he groaned as he lowered his gaze to her breasts and her dusky nipples. Hunger bolted through him and he couldn't stop himself from dropping his head and capturing her right nipple. Her moan was sweet and sultry at the same time as he suckled it, licked and nipped at it.

He slid one hand around her back, settling it on her bottom, and stroked his other hand down through her damp folds. She was slick for him, warm and wet, enticing. He groaned against her breast, dipped down to her warm core and eased his finger deep into her, gaining another long moan from her that had his cock aching, hungry to be inside her.

She moaned again and threaded her fingers into his hair, loosening it from its ponytail and clutching him to her breast. He licked her nipple, swirling his tongue around the hard bead, and slowly pumped her with his finger, loving the feel of her warm velvet depths around it. He stroked the soft spot inside her, running his finger around it, applying enough pressure to make her gasp and cling to him.

The moment she tightened around him, he pulled his finger out and stopped touching her. She whined and ran her hands down his neck and over his wings.

A shiver bolted through him when she clutched them, holding him to her with them, her grip so tight it felt as though she wasn't going to let him go.

He kissed up from her breasts to her neck, licking and sucking it, drawing a mixture of giggles and moans from her. She stilled when he took hold of his cock and ran it down through her folds, and sighed as he eased himself into her, stretching her tight body.

"Apollyon." She kissed him, still holding his wings, clinging to him.

Her kiss slowed but grew passionate, dominant in a way that he hadn't expected from her—a way that thrilled him.

He took hold of her hips and held her steady as he slowly thrust into her, long strokes that would have him coming undone before long, but the sound of her moaning into his mouth was worth it. She kissed him deeper, her tongue tangling with his, her grip on his wings tight and unrelenting.

"Apollyon," she whispered against his lips between kisses, saying it with such hunger that he drove deeper into her, struggling to keep his pace slow.

He gathered her into his arms, kissing her, moving deep within her, feeling the intensity of their bodies fusing as one. He could sense her feelings, experienced the pleasure that radiated through her, throbbing in waves that crashed over him and threatened to carry him away with her.

It felt different to last night, almost overwhelming in the strength of emotion it evoked in him. Emotion that drove him to hold her closer, to clutch her to him as fiercely as she clutched him to her, and to never let her go.

She was everything he needed.

Air in his lungs.

Life in his breast.

She was everything.

He held her close, as close as he could get to her, seeking a stronger connection between them so he could know that this meant something to her too.

Her hands left his wings and she gripped his shoulders, drawing him closer still and wrapping her legs around his waist, until he could barely move inside her. He thrust shallow and slow, drawing the moment out, wanting it to last forever as her lips played over his, as gentle as their lovemaking, and he was lost.

He searched her feelings, trying to discover how she felt, needing to know what this meant to her.

It had to be more than lust. She had to want him too.

Need him too.

He sensed the moment he broke through whatever barrier Serenity had kept him at bay with, and her feelings flooded him, warm and full of affection, heating his heart until it felt as though it would melt.

He felt her confusion too, her growing feelings and how they frightened her.

They filled him, wrapped him in their embrace, until they joined with his.

Could she feel him too now?

He wanted her to. He opened himself to her so she wouldn't be afraid and would feel his emotions and know that she wasn't alone. He felt something for her too. This was more than lust and hunger. This was something magical.

She buried her face into his neck and her fingers into his hair, holding him, clinging as though she never wanted this to end too.

Apollyon thrust deeper into her again, longer strokes that elicited breathy moans from her that washed over his skin. Her body tensed around his and he brought her right to the edge of the counter, clutching her backside to support her so she wouldn't fall, and drove harder into her. Her moans grew louder, and he groaned with her each time he plunged into her warm depths, searching for release, wanting to feel her climax.

She threw her head back and uttered his name as she came, her body quivering and clenching him, drawing him into joining her. Release rushed through him and he growled her name as a raw curse as he seated himself in her, clung to her as he throbbed and his entire body quaked from the force of his release.

He rested his head on her shoulder, breathing hard as he struggled to remain standing, sensation bombarding him and tangling him up inside. Serenity remained still in his arms, holding him, her body gently quivering around his. He could sense her nerves, that he wasn't the only one who wasn't sure what to do now, how to process the feelings growing inside him.

When he finally convinced himself to move, to draw back and look at her, she smiled shyly at him.

"I think we could use that shower now." A hint of colour climbed onto her cheeks.

He nodded, withdrew his cock from her, and set her down. She scurried off into the living room.

Apollyon went to follow her and then paused. He looked back at the coffee machine. The black contents of the glass jug called to him.

He smiled.

Perhaps he could use a lift before the shower.

He had done things slow, had drawn out her feelings for him and revealed his own. This time, he would unleash his passion again, the wild way she made him feel, because he had the feeling that she needed it again, needed to lose herself in the intensity of a shared moment, one where the only thing that mattered was finding pleasure in each other's arms. She needed time to come to terms with her feelings, and he would give it to her, wouldn't press her until she was sure of herself again.

He found a cup and poured some of the coffee into it. It was hot but it didn't stop him. He blew on it a few times and then sipped it. The effect was instantaneous. His cock twitched and he groaned at the thought of showering with Serenity. He took a mouthful of coffee, grimaced as he swallowed the hot liquid, and then went after her, his erection growing harder with each step.

She wasn't difficult to find. The shower was already running by the time he located the bathroom off the bedroom. He pushed the door open and stood there a moment, cock hard and aching at the sight of her as she stood under the jet of water running her hands over her bare body.

He wanted to do that for her.

He focused and forced his wings away, until they shrank and disappeared into his back. It wasn't good to get them wet. They took hours to dry.

As he stepped into the small shower cubicle, Serenity smiled and pushed her wet blonde hair back, slicking it against her head. There wasn't much room, but then he didn't need it for what he was planning.

He took the soap from her, lathered it onto his hands, and ran them over her slender body. The slippery supple feel of her beneath his palms was incredible. He washed her sides and then continued down to the apex of her thighs, the soap rinsing off his hands under the warm spray of water. She moaned when he slipped his fingers into her folds and found her nub, teasing it with his fingers.

The feel of her was enough to have him hard as steel, aching painfully.

Damn, he wanted her.

Wasn't sure he would ever stop needing her so fiercely.

She opened her mouth when he lifted her and he silenced her with a kiss, showing her that they didn't need to talk right now. Right now, they just needed to feel. Talking could come later.

She seemed to get the message. Her kiss grew desperate, her movements as choppy and wild as his own. He couldn't do slow and sexy this time. He needed to be inside her again and the way she was moaning into his mouth, her tongue tangling with his, and how aroused she still was said that he wasn't the only one in need.

Apollyon pinned her to the white tiles with his body, the shower spraying against his back, water running over his bare bottom and his thighs. Serenity opened her legs and wrapped them around his hips and he groaned, kissing her harder, pouring out the frantic hunger pounding in his veins into the kiss.

He held her with one hand, his strength making it easy for him to keep her there, and reached for his cock with his other. She moaned when he guided it to her opening and then thrust into her, deep and hard. Her hands flew to his shoulders, her fingernails pressing into his muscles, and he groaned and grabbed her hips as she worked them, rolling them in a maddening way.

Her tongue duelled with his, fighting for dominance that he wasn't going to give her this time. He held her hips, lifted her off his cock as he withdrew and then brought her down when he slammed back into her hot depths, claiming her body as his. He thrust fast and furious, plundering her body, driven by the raw hunger and the dark need spiralling inside him.

He had to have her.

She would be his.

He wouldn't let her go now, not ever.

She groaned with each deep thrust of his cock, each time he brought her down hard onto it, and clung to him, kissing him with a passion that matched his own.

It was rough and frantic, a chaotic meeting of their desire and passion, a raw primal fulfilling of their hunger for one another.

It was bliss.

She cried out when she climaxed, her body shivering against him and her warm silken core milking his cock. He buried his face in her neck, grunting with each deep plunge of his length into her, wanting to draw out each stroke until he couldn't take any more. She clenched her muscles around him, moaning hotly into his ear, and it was too much. He groaned and held her on him as he spilled, his heart pounding and his head spinning with it.

Heaven.

He had been in Hell for millennia, and now he had found Heaven.

And he wouldn't give her up.

He needed her too much.

# CHAPTER 11

Serenity felt sore in all the good places and all the right ways. She walked beside Apollyon on the wide pavement of the Champs Elysees, holding his hand and grinning like an idiot.

How did he make her smile so easily?

It wasn't the sex. That was fantastic but it wasn't the reason she couldn't stop smiling. It was just him. She only had to look at him and she smiled again, even against her will.

He was looking ahead, watching the people coming towards them, the traffic, everything. It all seemed to interest him. When she had been looking up at his handsome profile for a minute, he turned his head and looked down at her. He smiled and her heart fluttered in her throat.

He needed a licence for that smile.

The effect it had on her was definitely illegal.

She turned her gaze away from him, looking up at the dark sky. It was a beautiful night and even though the stars were faint, she felt as though she was seeing them shining above her.

Her smile finally faltered when she dropped her eyes to the street again.

They were almost at the end of the long shopping avenue, near the Louvre, and she sighed as the sight of it dampened her mood.

She didn't want to go and confront Edward again but Apollyon had insisted on doing his duty to her and they were searching for him, using a tracking spell she had put together using an item he had left behind in her apartment.

An item that would hopefully lead her to him so she could reclaim the ones he had stolen from her.

It was the only reason she had agreed to go along with Apollyon's plan to continue his mission. She didn't want to see Edward again, no longer felt angry about what he had done or hurt by it. She just wanted to move on with her life now that it was looking up again.

But to do that, she needed closure, and she would never have it if she didn't get the books back.

Serenity snuck a glance at Apollyon. She was glad that she could see through his glamour. He had assured her that he was wearing a dark suit again, although she could only see his beautiful black and gold armour. The sight of him in so little did have its drawbacks now that she had gotten over her reserve about him though.

It made her want to take him into a dark alley and have her very wicked way with him.

He grinned, as though he knew what she was thinking, and cast his blue gaze over her. The hunger in it told her that he was thinking the same thing she was. She had picked out her best dark blue summer dress and coupled it with the bra that gave her the most cleavage. She wanted Apollyon's eyes on her tonight. She needed to have him looking at her, boosting her confidence with the way his attention seemed to gravitate towards her all the time, and the way he looked as though he wanted to eat her up.

Something about him had brought her to life, freeing her inhibitions. She had never been so adventurous with a man, and had never felt so beautiful or adored. Being with Apollyon was Heaven.

She guessed that it was probably the angel effect.

She shifted her focus back to her spell as they turned and walked down a road that led away from the Louvre and the river, and deeper into the city.

Edward was around here somewhere.

It took them a while to find his location and she could only stare at the pink neon sign above the door when they did.

It wasn't the sort of club that she had imagined it would be.

She had never been to an exotic dance club before. She presumed it meant exactly what her mind conjured up. Lap dancing. Erotic acts on stage. All manner of sordid things.

All of which felt like a very bad thing to expose an angel to, even one who had probably done worse with her over the past twenty-four hours.

"Problem?" Apollyon's deep voice was music to her ears, warming her body through as quickly as the images of them together that had been popping into her head.

"It's a strip club." She pointed to the sign.

"How about we go in and just see if he's there?" He didn't seem at all bothered by that as he led her towards the doors and the man let them through again without even blinking, and without making them pay.

Apollyon had some powers and he wasn't afraid to use them. She wished she felt so confident about her own powers. Her mother had always told her that she had great power and could do anything she desired if she trained hard enough. She had never felt confident enough to face her powers and accept them.

Now she was though.

Being with Apollyon gave her the strength to stop hiding and to take the leap. She wanted to be a better witch and master them and she would.

He ducked as they passed under a low beam and she smiled. His head would have cleared it but his folded wings would have clipped it. She couldn't imagine how strange he had looked to everyone else, ducking when he didn't need to.

A few women immediately closed in on him, dressed in skimpy underwear and wide smiles, all of them regular humans as far as she could tell.

Apollyon pulled her up level with him and she felt awkward when the women noticed her and the grip he had on her hand and moved away again, heading towards other men who were alone.

That awkwardness faded when he glanced down at her, the heat in his blue eyes reassuring her that he wasn't interested in the other women or what anyone in the club thought as he strode through it holding her hand.

Did he want everyone to know that they were together? Did he want to be with her?

Being with him last night and today had been incredible and had only made her want him even more, but she still wasn't sure where this was all going to lead and whether it would end up the way she wanted it to in her heart.

Her pleasant dream about them staying together disappeared when she spotted Edward was right in front of her with a group of people, half of which were pretty young women. He raked his fingers through his short light brown hair and spoke to one of the men beside him, a smile on his lips and a sparkle in his dark eyes as he watched the dancers on the stage near him. His black shirt hugged his chest, revealing his slim figure, one she had appreciated before but one that did nothing for her now.

Apollyon's athletic physique, his clear blue eyes and the sculpted planes of his face, and his long black hair did everything for her though.

She glanced at the stage and regretted it when she got an eyeful of bottom as one of the pole-dancers twirled and gyrated. She dragged her eyes away, her cheeks blazing, and looked at Apollyon, expecting to find him watching the women like the other men in the club.

His focus was on her, his blue gaze intent and instantly meeting hers.

"Do you want to leave?" He frowned and touched her cheek with his free hand, caressing it softly and soothing her nerves.

Shaking her head, she searched for her courage and a place where they would be noticed by Edward but not everyone else. She didn't want Apollyon looking at the other women. It was childish of her, but she wanted him all to herself.

"We should leave." He went to but she stopped him, holding his hand in both of hers. He looked back at her. "You are not happy here."

"Just... I..." She bit her lip, looked deep into his eyes and tried to find the words she wanted to say to him. "Don't look at the women."

It was easier than she had thought it would be.

He smiled and cocked his head. "Afraid you will corrupt me or get me into trouble?"

"No." She looked down at his hand where she held it. "It's not that at all."

Apollyon stepped back to her and cupped her cheek with his free hand, and then raised it, bringing her head up with it so she had no choice but to look into his eyes. There was so much understanding in them.

She hadn't wanted him to know her fear, that she was afraid he might leave her for one of the beautiful women in the room, that she might lose him. She didn't know what her feelings for him were, but the thought of him with another woman cut her deep, right down into her heart, and she had needed to ask him.

Being here had made her realise something though.

Whatever she felt for him, she wanted him to stick around when all of this was over.

She didn't want him to leave.

She closed her eyes when he kissed her, a soft one full of reassurance and tenderness. His hand shifted in hers and he held it tightly. She followed him across the room, towards the booths that lined the wall opposite the area where Edward was sitting, directly in his line of sight.

Hopefully he would notice her and it would be enough to satisfy Apollyon and the first part of his mission—making her ex jealous.

She wasn't sure how he planned to fulfil the other part of it, but something about the way his eyes darkened whenever he glanced Edward's way said it was going to involve force.

Apollyon was a warrior, but part of her didn't want him to fight. Not because she didn't like violence, but because she didn't want him to get hurt. He was powerful, but Edward could use curses and spells to weaken him and make him vulnerable.

Apollyon held his other hand out and smiled, and she slid into the dark leather horseshoe seat. He settled himself beside her, his attention wholly on her, and she thanked him with a kiss.

She hadn't meant it to be anything more than a brief meeting of lips, but he kissed her back, his tongue tracing a line along the seam of her lips. She opened for him, inviting his tongue into her mouth with her own, stroking his and drawing a moan from him. He moved closer to her on the seat, until they were hip to hip.

It still wasn't close enough.

He grinned when she pushed the round table away to make room and then sat on his lap, so her bottom rested on his thighs, her knees tucked up near his left hip, and her arms were around his neck. Their tongues tangled and he moaned when she ran hers lightly over his lower lip, teasing him with it. He slid his hands around her waist and she moved hers down to his arms, loving the feel of his rock hard biceps beneath her wandering fingers.

The club disappeared, everything drifting away until it felt as though they were the only two in the world, kissing and touching each other, reigniting the flames of their passion and need.

Serenity had never felt so alive, so full of desire.

Apollyon pulled her closer and pushed his hand up over her stomach to her breasts. He cupped one, earning a moan from her, and kissed her deep and slow, gently stoking the fire burning within her, steadily building it into an inferno that she was going to beg him to quench.

Someone stopped near them and she stared wide-eyed up at the barely-dressed dark-haired woman. Apollyon frowned and waved his hand. The woman nodded and walked away.

"What did you do?" Serenity avoided his kisses.

He uttered a dark sound of frustration and tried to kiss her again. When she evaded him a second time, he sighed and leaned back into the leather chair.

The bright lights of the club flashed across his face, leaving the right side of his profile in darkness. The music was louder than she had noticed on first entering and there seemed to be more people now, some of which were staring in their direction. She was probably giving them a free show. Kissing was as far as it went though. She wasn't about to publicly expose herself and ride Apollyon, no matter how much she wanted it.

"I compelled her to get us some drinks."

Drinks sounded good. She let him kiss her again and snuck a glance in Edward's direction.

One of the men at his table was watching them. She recognised him as another from his coven, which meant they had moved to Paris as Edward had told her they were going to and her coven's books were probably already in their hands. Damn it.

She needed to get them back, and she was starting to consider doing it herself.

The confidence Apollyon had awoken in her was a more potent drug than she had realised, filled with her resolve and strength she had never known before. She was no longer the meek witch who lived in fear of messing things up whenever she tried using her powers. She had cast a tracking spell without it going wrong. She could use the other spells she had memorised to force Edward to return what he had stolen from her.

But first, she intended to make the bastard sick with jealousy.

She closed her eyes and lost herself in Apollyon's hungry kisses again, wrapping her arms around his neck and stroking his feathers. He groaned and she did it again. She had realised back on her balcony that he liked it when she touched his wings, and whenever they had been out since then, she had found herself wanting to caress them.

The black feathers were softest near his shoulders where they entered slits in his chest armour, like silk beneath her fingers, and each sweep of her hands elicited another moan from him and turned his kisses hotter, until he was devouring her mouth with each one. His left hand settled on her breast, thumbing her nipple through the thin material of her dress.

Heat pooled at the apex of her thighs and she wriggled on his lap, shifting her legs together to make the most of the feeling there.

She wished they were back at her apartment right now, on her couch, or anywhere that she could take it beyond kissing and groping. She wasn't sure she would ever get enough of her dark angel.

Apollyon's hands wandered down, his right kneading her bottom and his left creeping up her thigh, drawing the flared skirt of her dress back. She moaned and tackled his tongue with hers, kissing him with desperate need and encouraging him to go as far as they could in public.

Someone was standing near them again.

She broke the kiss, expecting to find the waitress there, and her eyes flew wide.

Edward stood before her.

Apollyon casually leaned back and stroked her thigh in lazy lengths, running his fingertips back and forth along it.

"Serenity?" Edward said with an air of disbelief that matched the shock on his face.

"Pig?" She stared at him. He didn't leave. "Can I help you with something? Perhaps you came to return my books?"

"Yes... you could help me with something." Edward lunged forwards and grabbed her wrist. He tugged but Apollyon wrapped his arms around her waist, holding her in place on his lap. Edward smiled thinly. "I just want to talk."

"Talk?" She glared at him and muttered a spell beneath her breath, and Edward yelped and withdrew his hands. Tiny sparks of electricity leaped between his fingers as he shook them. "You want to talk? I want my books back."

Edward continued to stare at her, his dark gaze dropping to her exposed thigh every so often. She smoothed her dress over her legs and surprise rolled through her when Apollyon set her down on the couch beside him.

He stood and faced Edward.

Edward glared right back at him, his already dark eyes blackening further as he tipped his chin up and straightened his spine, trying to appear taller.

Even then he fell short of Apollyon's towering height, was forced to look up at him.

Serenity sat very still, afraid of moving and breaking whatever battle of wills was happening between them. When neither looked as though they were going to back down or say anything, she rose from the seat and stepped between them.

"We have nothing to talk about, Edward." The confident edge to her voice pleased her.

She had thought that it would shake and give away her rising nerves.

She wasn't sure what to do or what to say. Here was her big chance to look Edward in the eye and tell him what a bastard he had been to her by cheating on her and how she wanted him to suffer but she couldn't find the strength to confront him, not even with Apollyon at her back.

Edward stepped towards her, his dark look shifting to reveal a charming smile. She had fallen for that smile before and it wasn't going to happen again. He had broken her heart, had betrayed her, and she would never forgive him for it, and she would never believe a word he said because of it.

"I've never seen you like this, Serenity... so passionate... sensual... just talk to me. I was a fool, I made a mistake... I never realised just how good you were for me." Edward reached out to her and she stared at his hand, her heart beating painfully against her ribs. "I want you back. I'll give you your books and we'll be good again."

Serenity looked into his eyes. He was being honest. She didn't need a spell to see that. Why though? Why was he suddenly interested in her again when he hadn't even looked back when she had dumped him for cheating on her?

"Just talk to me." Edward smiled. "I want you back... I'll do anything."

The books he had stolen from her appeared in his hands.

"You want these don't you?" He held them out to her and she was tempted to reach for them.

Cold crept through her when she sensed Apollyon step back, away from her, as though he thought she had already made her decision and was going to leave.

Edward had cheated on her. He had betrayed her trust. He had hurt her so badly that she had asked for revenge and Apollyon had given it to her and so much more.

He had fixed her heart.

He had brought her smile back and made her feel alive again.

Was that what Edward was seeing now? Were the feelings Apollyon had brought to life in her, the happiness and the passion, what he wanted from her? She couldn't give that to him. He had never made her feel as Apollyon did.

Serenity looked over her shoulder at Apollyon, right into his blue eyes, and saw his feelings in them. The same look shone in their depths that had been there earlier when they had been in the kitchen and he had said that he had been alone for too long. He didn't want to be alone anymore.

He wanted to be with her.

It all seemed so impossible, so ridiculous, but she wanted to be with him too and she knew in her heart the reason why.

She was falling for him.

She was falling in love with an angel.

# CHAPTER 12

Serenity felt like a bitch when she took a step towards Edward and Apollyon tensed behind her. She hadn't meant to make him believe that she was going to leave him for the bastard stood before her.

Victory flashed in Edward's smile, but it was short lived.

She placed her hands on the books he held and looked him right in the eyes as she teleported them away, leaving him empty handed.

She kept her gaze locked on his and stepped back, until Apollyon's body was against hers again. Relief washed through her, warmth that chased the cold that had been building in her heart away and reassured her as he wrapped his strong arms around her from behind, linking his hands over her chest, holding her flush against him, so close that she felt he wouldn't let her go.

She didn't want him to.

She wanted him to hold on to her forever.

"I don't love you anymore," she said to Edward with all the conviction she felt in her heart and shook her head. "You're a bastard and I hope you feel as lousy as I did."

She closed her eyes when Apollyon pressed a kiss to her bare shoulder.

Edward cursed at her and Apollyon held her closer as she flinched away, expecting a direct hit with the spell behind his words but feeling nothing.

Because of Apollyon?

Could his power shield her from magic?

She sought the comfort of his embrace and how safe it made her feel, and opened her eyes and cursed back at Edward with all of her heart. She wasn't brave enough to curse him properly, condemning him as Apollyon would, but she did manage to work her way through several sexually transmitted diseases before she got the better of herself and stopped.

Serenity coolly held Edward's gaze. He glared at her, and then at Apollyon.

"You did this to her," he spat the words at Apollyon, his eyes dark with accusation. "You changed her."

"I only made her happy." Apollyon pressed another light kiss to her shoulder. "It is all I want for her."

Edward's eyes met hers again. "You think he loves you? I know his type, Serenity, and as soon as he's bored with you, he'll move on to someone better."

Serenity stepped out of Apollyon's arms and up to Edward. He could curse her all he wanted, but she was damned if she was going to let him bad mouth Apollyon.

"He is *nothing* like you." She held his gaze, unafraid of the darkness in his eyes, feeling safe and strong with Apollyon so close to her.

It was spiteful of Edward to say such things about Apollyon and to try to turn her against him and plant seeds of doubt into her head. Apollyon would never betray her. He had seen how much Edward had hurt her and had come to take her pain away, and at the same time had made her feel more loved than she ever had.

Edward looked as though he was going to say something and then stormed away, heading back towards the table where his friends waited. The dark looks several of them sent her had her nerves rising again. Edward she could probably handle, but if his friends decided to fight in his corner, she wouldn't be able to defend herself against their combined magic.

Serenity turned, stepped into Apollyon's waiting embrace and looked up at him. He placed his hands on her upper arms and then slid them around her, holding her close.

"I think I hurt him enough. Let's go home." She plastered on a smile to cover her fear and waited for him to agree.

Only he didn't.

He just stared down at her, and the longer he looked at her, the stronger the fear inside her grew.

Because his eyes were changing.

They were bluer than normal and the pale flecks began to brighten as she stared at them, until his eyes were almost glowing. His jaw tensed and he looked over her head towards Edward's table.

"Not yet," he muttered and moved her aside.

She placed herself in front of him again, arms outstretched to block his path. "What are you doing?"

"Having *my* vengeance." He looked down at her. "Do not worry. I will settle this in a mortal way and with mortal strength. My powers were limited the moment I decided to fight a human."

She still didn't like the sound of that and she wasn't about to let him get into a fight because of her. She had no doubt that he could best Edward in a fight done in a human way, but Edward wasn't going to set aside his magic in order to let that happen. He would use spells against Apollyon.

Apollyon evaded her when she tried to grab his arms and strode past her, heading straight for Edward on the other side of the low-lit club. Edward stood as Apollyon approached and Serenity hurried to keep up with him, darting through the waitresses and patrons.

Before Edward could even finish standing, Apollyon launched his right fist at him, caught him hard across the jaw, and sent him crashing to the ground.

Serenity gasped and stared at Edward, afraid that Apollyon had been wrong about his powers being limited. Edward groaned and rubbed his cheek as he pushed onto his feet.

His eyes darkened, narrowing on Apollyon.

She sensed the hum of magic rising around him and his friends. She had to do something.

Panic lit her veins and she hastily called one of the books Edward had stolen back to her. The second it landed in her hands, she opened it, seeking one of the spells she had read in it. A defensive ward.

Her hands shook as she quickly flipped pages, heart racing and mind spinning.

Her eyes widened and she went back a few pages, slammed her finger against the page and uttered the words. The spell was beyond anything she had attempted before, and there was a high chance it was going to go terribly wrong, as most of her spells did, but she had to help Apollyon.

Edward raised his left hand and a blue glow surrounded it, growing brighter by the second.

When she whispered the last word, his focus snapped to her.

Too late.

The magic that had been gathering around his hand stuttered and died, locked down by the spell. She wobbled on her feet as all of her strength flowed out of her, drained by a combination of casting the spell and fear of messing things up and failing to protect Apollyon.

She sank to her knees on the tacky floor.

Apollyon looked back over his shoulder at her, concern written across his face, the brightness of his eyes fading as he turned towards her.

Giving his back to Edward.

Edward launched himself at Apollyon, who ducked out of reach of the punch, twisted at the waist to face him again and came back with a solid left of his own. Edward stumbled backwards and Apollyon advanced, his larger build making Edward look tiny in comparison.

Apollyon's wings blocked her view of his next attack. She didn't want to watch but couldn't tear her eyes away as they fought, both landing punches and grabbing at each other. Edward's friends didn't seem to know what to do either. They all stood to one side, crowded around the table, gazes darting between the fight and her. None of them looked inclined to attempt to use their magic to intervene. Were they afraid she would cast a spell on them next, stripping them of their powers for a few days?

She didn't have the strength left to cast another spell like that, was sure it would take days to recover her own magic too, but she wasn't going to tell them that.

She slowly gathered the strength to pull herself back onto her feet, because she didn't want to think about what sort of disgusting things were on the floor beneath her. She clutched a nearby chair and hauled herself up as Apollyon dodged another blow. Edward made a low noise in his throat and followed with a second punch, and this one caught Apollyon on his chest.

Which didn't affect him in the slightest since it struck the armour hidden by his glamour, but it did have Edward cursing and grimacing as he clutched his hand.

"You cheating son of a bitch," Edward bit out.

"Takes one to know one." Apollyon advanced, his steps sure and measured, closing in on Edward.

"What the fuck are you?" Edward backed off a step, sizing Apollyon up, and Apollyon must have done something that allowed him to see his true appearance, because all the colour suddenly drained from her ex's face and his eyes widened, a flicker of fear dancing in them.

Serenity turned towards the doors of the club when she sensed danger. Three burly men dressed in smart black clothing were coming at them fast. Security. She turned back in time to see Apollyon slam his right fist into

Edward's stomach, causing him to double up, and then strike him hard across the jaw with a left hook.

Edward hit the dirty club floor and sprawled out, his face covered in gashes.

"Stay away from Serenity," Apollyon growled and loomed over Edward.

The security team shoved past her, knocking her into the table, and grabbed Apollyon before she could reach him. Apollyon didn't take his eyes off Edward as they dragged him towards the exit. Her gaze followed him and widened when she saw the blood and cuts on his face.

Why had he fought Edward? She'd had her revenge and she had reclaimed the books Edward had taken. That was all she had wanted.

Yes. All she had wanted.

This bloody mess born of violence was what Apollyon had wanted. He had avenged her in his own way, as a warrior.

Her eyes roamed back to Edward where he lay unconscious on the floor. They had both had their vengeance on Edward. She couldn't be angry with Apollyon. He had only fought Edward because he felt something for her and had wanted to protect her, to make sure that Edward left her alone.

He was braver than she was. In her heart, she had wanted to hurt Edward and punish him, and Apollyon had done that for her. As much as she didn't like violence, she was glad that he had fought, because it had not only given her the closure she had needed, but it had made his feelings for her clear.

Edward's friends surrounded him as she turned away and walked towards the door, following Apollyon. Each step she took away from Edward lifted the clouds from her heart. Each step she took towards Apollyon filled it with light.

The night was still warm when she stepped out of the club.

Her eyes darted around, seeking Apollyon. He paced a short distance from the three men guarding the club door, taking long clipped strides along the pavement in front of a row of parked cars. She could sense his agitation and desire. He wasn't satisfied. He had wanted the fight between him and Edward to last longer.

He looked up as she approached and then turned away.

The moment her hand came to rest on his shoulder, sliding over it, and she rounded him, he looked across at her. Her brow furrowed when she saw the cuts on his face. He hadn't lied to her. Heaven had stripped him of his power when he had decided to attack an innocent mortal, leaving him with only human strength. That power was back now, flowing into her body through her hand where it rested on his warm bare skin.

Serenity raised her other hand, cupped his cheek, and met his dark eyes. The low light stole the colour from his irises but something told her they were still lighter, full of burning energy as they had been in the club. She held his gaze and focused on him, on feeling his pain and where he had been hurt so she could fix it all. The spell she had cast on Edward had drained her, but she would use what little power she had left to take care of Apollyon.

The cuts on his face slowly healed, leaving only blood behind.

"Thank you." Apollyon's hand caught hers and he interlocked their fingers, holding them tightly.

He walked a short distance with her and then stopped at the start of the square at the end of the Champs Elysees.

"Do you want to talk to Edward?" he said in a low voice, so quiet that she thought she was hearing things until he looked at her, right into her eyes.

"No." She could see that it was a reach for reassurance and she faced him, took hold of his other hand and tried to give him what he needed. It was strange to have to reassure such a strong man but it was touching too. It made her realise that she wasn't alone in her feelings. They were both afraid but knowing that they were in this together took away some of her fear. "I've had enough of revenge. It's over. I just want to go home now."

He looked down at his feet, his expression distant. "Home."

Serenity looked there too. She knew what he was thinking and she didn't want him to leave her. She trembled on the brink of asking him to stay, to remain with her on Earth just as the other angels had done for the women they loved. He had proven himself loyal to his duty though and asking him to remain with her would probably be asking him to commit a great sacrifice.

And what if he said no?

She started when soft fingers touched her cheek, caressing the curve of her jaw.

"I will come home with you tonight... if that is acceptable?" he whispered and pressed a kiss to her forehead.

Serenity closed her eyes and nodded. She drew back and her eyes met his.

And tomorrow?

She couldn't bring herself to say it. The thought of him leaving weighed her down inside.

How could she convince him to stay when she couldn't find her voice to say the words?

She wasn't brave enough to admit her feelings, not after what had happened with Edward.

He reached for her and paused, his entire body tensing, and suddenly turned to look back the way they had come. She looked there too, catching a glimpse of a silver-haired woman being ushered into a black limousine. Her gaze roamed back to Apollyon and her eyebrows dipped low as she found him still staring at her, something that looked like surprise filling his eyes.

"Do you know her?" Serenity wanted to hear him say that he didn't even when she could see that he did, because the woman was beautiful, ethereal in a way.

Was she a female angel?

Apollyon nodded slowly, distant from her.

"Is she an angel?" Serenity watched the car as it pulled away. She hadn't felt any power in the woman, not as she could in Apollyon. She didn't even feel it when she fixed her focus on the car as it passed close to them.

She felt magic.

"There are no female angels," he muttered, gaze following the car. "A witch... she was a witch."

"A witch? When you mentioned having met a witch before... was she the one?" She had felt magic in the vehicle, but she wasn't sure it had come from the woman. She turned away as Apollyon nodded and focused on the car, but didn't have the strength to cast a spell that would allow her to detect which of the people in the vehicle possessed magic. She paused as she went to look back at Apollyon. "Wait. *Was* a witch?"

He blinked and looked down at her, a troubled edge to his expression. "I thought she was dead."

"What made you think that?" The woman had looked very much alive to Serenity, although there had been something off about her, something that she couldn't quite place her finger on.

"An angel I was close to... I thought him dead, but then I saw him in Hell." He looked back over his shoulder in the direction the car had gone. "I believed that the only reason Rook would fall was that she had been killed."

Serenity's eyes slowly widened as the strange sensation she'd had about the woman grew clearer and she had a flash of what she had seen.

"I think I know the people who were with her." She hoped she was wrong though. "My coven sent out a warning and the grapevine is full of stories about them."

"About who?" Apollyon's blue eyes dropped to her again, and they were definitely brighter again, filled with a need to know.

"Some sort of circle that has been taking witches, doing something with them. I think the man who was holding her arm matches the description my coven were given of one of the people behind the disappearances."

His eyes grew brighter still, the paler flecks swirling against their dark backdrop. He wanted to fight again.

"I'll help you find them." Because that way, he would stay with her a little longer.

"It's dangerous." He frowned down at her.

Serenity shook her head. "I'm stronger now. I can handle it... and I want to help you, Apollyon."

He looked as if he wasn't sure how to respond to that.

Had no one ever helped him before? Not even his friends?

The one he had called Rook, or the others he hadn't seen in some time?

He had said that he had been their team leader. Was it possible he was more accustomed to helping others than having others help him because of his position?

She stepped towards him, closing the gap between them, lifted her hand and placed it against his cheek, her eyes locking with his. "Let me help you, Apollyon."

He hesitated for only a heartbeat before he nodded.

Relief poured through her, lifting her heart again, because now she would be able to spend more time with him.

Apollyon scooped her up into his arms, cradling her, and smiled. "It is a nice night for a flight."

Serenity looked up at the dark sky. It was still clear. It was a nice night for flying, but she felt as though she was falling. She leaned her head against Apollyon's shoulder, holding his neck with one hand and his breastplate with the other, not wanting to let him go.

He hadn't said what happened next, and she had seen his reluctance to place her in danger in his eyes, and feared that if she let him go, he would hunt for the witch alone.

She was afraid that this would be the last time that she flew with him.

She was terrified she would never see him again.

# CHAPTER 13

Apollyon beat his black feathered wings and took off with Serenity, carrying her high above the roofs of the old buildings that lined the Champs Elysees. The Louvre shone in the distance, the pyramid golden and the windows of the older classical stone building still full of warm light.

He turned with Serenity and flew towards the Eiffel Tower at a slow pace, enjoying the feel of her in his arms and the warm summer breeze against his face.

She was quiet, nestled in his arms, deep in thought. Distant from him.

He didn't want to disturb her, so he carried her, cradling her close, careful with his precious cargo. He wasn't sure what to do. She wanted to help him, but he wasn't even sure he would be allowed to pursue that mission. He wasn't free to do as he pleased.

The city passed below him, a stream of lights and noises, and he kept his focus on the distant tower, considering everything that Serenity had said.

She had relieved him of his duty, even if she didn't know it.

She had told him it was over.

Now, he could only remain with her for so long. His position protecting the bottomless pit in Hell would call him back there whether he liked it or not. Without a reason to remain on Earth, a duty to fulfil there, he would have to return.

Even though he didn't want to go back.

Apollyon glanced at her out of the corner of his eye, wishing he could see her properly and that she would speak to him. The air felt heavy, hard to fly through, and he ached inside with a need to stay with her.

She looped her arms around his neck and it struck him that neither of them knew what to say.

Not even flying past the Eiffel Tower drew a reaction from her tonight. She didn't smile. She remained with her head on his shoulder, her breathing slow and soft, and her fingers still against his neck.

He wanted her to smile again.

He wanted things to be as they had before Edward had spoken to her.

Apollyon flew higher, leaving the world behind and seeking the silence he could only find when he was looking down on Earth from the skies far above.

Serenity held him tighter and curled up in his arms.

"I will never let you go," he whispered close to her forehead and held her safe in his arms. He stopped his ascent and hovered above Paris, his broad wings beating slowly, just fast enough to keep him stationary. "You do not need to fear, Serenity. I would catch you if you fell."

She pulled away from him and he adjusted his grip on her, holding her side so she didn't slip from his arms. Her hazel eyes were wide but he knew it wasn't because she was trying to see him in the low light. It was because she was surprised that one of them had found the courage to say what needed to be said.

"Would you?" Her eyes searched his.

He knew what she was asking.

He nodded. "I would. If you took the leap, I would catch you."

He drew her closer to him, so she was safer, and looked deep into her eyes.

"My duty is done... I will have to return." His voice grew tight and he frowned as need collided inside him, a thousand dreams he wasn't sure would come true. "I wish it did not have to be this way though."

She shook her head. "No. Can't you stay a little longer?"

"How long?"

She smiled and softly whispered, "How about forever?"

"It sounds wonderful." He pressed a kiss to her lips and then sighed as he pulled away from her again, his eyes meeting hers. "But it is not that easy for me to leave Hell."

"I take it back then." Her grip on his shoulders tightened, her desperation flowing into him through her touch to mingle with his own. "My vengeance isn't done."

Apollyon shook his head, sorrow beating inside him as he held her closer again and he wished she could mend everything so easily. "It does not work that way. The contract is broken."

Paris stretched out before them over one hundred foot below, the lights twinkling and bright, all of it on display for Serenity, but her eyes were on him, laced with tears now that tore at him. He wanted her to smile again. He wanted her to be happy. He wanted to love her and be with her.

If he could, he would bring her here every night if she asked that of him. He would do anything for her.

His eyes gradually widened.

Drifted to her.

"Call to me."

"Apollyon?" she said with a confused crinkle between her fine eyebrows.

"No. Call to me..." His eyes darted between hers and his pulse quickened.

It could work.

His fellow warriors had to have done something similar to change their allegiance from their master to the object of their love. They couldn't have just quit. Angels didn't get that sort of choice. Damn it, maybe they did. Some must have forsaken their wings. Others must have found a loophole or something that allowed them to remain on Earth and serve there instead.

He could do neither of those things. His duty was eternal, unbreakable. He had been born with a purpose and he couldn't deny it.

His life was servitude, spent as his master commanded.

But perhaps it was possible for him to retain his eternal duty and serve a different master instead.

Serenity had commanded him to help her gain revenge. She could command him to be hers.

"Like you did before at the fountain when we met. Wish for me or whatever you did." He desperately searched her eyes. "Tell me to be with you forever, until you no longer need my services."

Serenity closed her eyes and held her hands over her heart. A pale light began to glow there, steadily growing in strength until it lit her hands and her face, and shone on him too. Magic. It was how he had heard her call. Her power had amplified her voice and his feelings for her had made him be the one to respond.

Apollyon watched her, listening to everything, desperate to hear her call again and to answer it. It was quiet at first, as it had been when he had been in Hell, but then he felt it within him, beating in his heart, compelling him to obey.

He seized it, greedily accepted it and swiftly responded to it before it could fade or slip through his fingers.

He bound them by a contract that was unbreakable.

Eternal.

He was her warrior now, and forever.

"Look at me," he whispered.

The light in her hands faded and then winked out of existence.

"Did it work?" There was such a beautiful look of hope in her hazel eyes.

He smiled to see how much this meant to her and how much she wanted it.

He nodded. "What is your command?"

"To stay with me until the end of time." A smile curved her lips and he was glad to see it.

"I can do that." He didn't even stop to consider the implications of what he was doing.

His old master would find someone else to guard the bottomless pit. There were at least a dozen angels who wanted the position more than he did now. He was tired of being in Hell. He wanted to stay here in Heaven with Serenity.

Apollyon kissed her, slowly and lightly, a bare meeting of lips that warmed him through from his heart outwards. Her hands came to rest on his shoulders and she kissed him back, her lips soft against his, and slid her arms around his neck. He beat his wings and flew with her, spiralling down towards Earth and smiling while he kissed her.

She clung to him in a way that he would never grow tired of and would always adore. It wasn't fear that made her hold him so tightly. It was love. They were both falling.

Spreading his wings, he carried them upwards again, over the rooftops of Paris.

As the sounds of the world drifted around them, Serenity broke away from his lips and looked out over the city. He focused on her, eyes tracing her profile as she gazed at the city.

She was smiling again, her eyes twinkling with the happiness that he could feel in her, and he couldn't help smiling too.

He didn't need to look to find the way back to her place now. It was so much easier to find things from above and once he had flown somewhere, he rarely forgot the way. He watched her instead, using his senses to guide him to her apartment.

When they were close, he looked for her apartment and swooped down to land gently on the black metal railing around the balcony. He stepped onto the tiles with her and set her down on her feet.

He folded his wings and focused on them, forcing them away. They went reluctantly, disappearing into his back.

Serenity stroked his bare arms, her eyes on his shoulders. They lifted to meet his and there was a note of sadness in their hazel depths.

"Will you have to lose your wings?" She looked as if she didn't want that to happen, as if the thought he might truly saddened her.

Which brought a small smile to his lips.

When she had first met him only two days ago, she had been afraid of his wings and what they represented. Now she looked as though she wanted them back this instant.

"No." He ran his fingers through her long blonde hair, enjoying the silky feel of it. "If I did that, I would not be able to take you flying."

She pressed her hands against his chest armour, tiptoed, and kissed him.

"You make me feel as though I'm flying when my feet are firmly on the ground," she whispered against his lips and he kissed her again, harder this time, stirring the passion that burned so fiercely between them.

He wasn't sure it would ever fade, felt certain it would always blaze so brightly, threatening to consume him at any moment.

"If you are flying now, then how will you feel in a minute?" He swept her back into his arms, carrying her into the apartment.

She giggled and kissed him, her mouth warm and sweet against his, pushing at his control. He wanted to lay her down right there in the kitchen and make love with her.

"Wait." She wriggled out of his arms and pulled him back to the balcony.

She grinned and kissed him again. He frowned but didn't stop her. What was she up to?

His eyebrows rose as she tiptoed and started to unbuckle his breastplate.

"Here?" He cast a glance around at the small balcony and then to the ones either side. They were all dark, with a small solid wall and section of the roof between them, but it didn't mean that someone wasn't going to walk out and see them.

"No one will see us." Serenity undid the first of the buckles and smiled wickedly at him. "If you won't hide us, then I can."

He hadn't thought of that. He could easily mask them from mortal eyes as long as he was concentrating.

Serenity swept her hands across his collarbones to his other shoulder and a hot shiver cascaded down his spine and tripped over his chest, causing his eyes to slip shut.

If he could concentrate anyway.

Serenity snapped her fingers and a thick padded blanket covered the balcony tiles beneath their feet.

If she wanted this moment to be romantic, he could help with that.

He focused and used his powers to make candles appear, lines of them along the walls and clusters in the corners of the balcony. Their flames burst into life, lighting the darkness with a warm glow that chased up Serenity's bare legs and shimmered in her golden hair.

She looked at the candles and then back at him. She clicked her fingers again and his clothes disappeared.

Two could play this game.

Her dress was gone in an instant, shortly followed by her high heels and then her underwear.

She gasped and covered herself.

Apollyon covered them both, masking them from mortal eyes, and pulled her flush against his bare body. He claimed her lips with his as he stroked his hands down her sides to her hips. Her skin was warm beneath his fingers and she shivered when he caressed her waist and then skimmed his hands around to her bottom. The feel of her belly against his hips stirred his cock.

He was about to kiss her again when she dropped to her knees in front of him and took his still-hardening length into her hot mouth.

Damn.

He swallowed hard as blood surged through him and his cock twitched as she sucked it to hardness. It ached and he ached with it, wanting to sheath himself in her again, knowing this time that he didn't have to leave her and that they would never be alone again because now they had each other.

When it became too much, he pushed her back so she released him and kneeled before her. He kissed her again and she eagerly accepted it, clutched his shoulders and leaned into it as her lips brushed his.

He pressed forwards, forcing her to lie down, and covered her with his body, groaned at the feel of her cushioning him as he kissed her. She moaned softly into his mouth and then rolled with him, so she was on top, and straddled his hips. All of his fight left him as he looked up at her.

He frowned as he ran his hands up her thighs, drinking in the stunning sight of her. She looked beautiful sitting on him, confidence sparkling in her hazel eyes, her body bare and open to him.

Serenity traced patterns on his chest with her fingertips, teasing his nipples before running them down towards his hips, drawing his attention there. Her warm heat covered his shaft, trapping it between their bodies, teasing and torturing him.

He rubbed against her, thrusting slowly through her slick folds, enjoying the feel of her astride him. Her eyes slipped shut and she leaned her head back. Her sweet low moan was too much for him, igniting a powerful need to be inside her. He wanted to hear her moan like that as he joined them, wanted her to ride him just as he had been aching for her to in the exotic club.

Her fingertips grazed the lines of his hips, ran around his navel and then up the valley between his abdominals. His gaze remained fixed on her face, absorbing the way she watched her fingers with hungry eyes. She splayed her hands out and swept them over his chest, her teeth tugging her lower lip at the same time, and then leaned over him.

Apollyon closed his eyes when her bare breasts brushed his stomach and slid his hands down her sides to her bottom. She ran her fingers into his long dark hair and brought her elbows to rest either side of his head. Her warm mouth found his, tongue sliding between his lips, and he moaned as she kissed him. It was slow and sweet, calming his urge to be inside her.

When she kissed him like this, he could wait forever.

It stole his attention and his heart.

He frowned when she moved away, kissing down his jaw and then his neck, over his chest. Her tongue swirled around his left nipple as she sank lower, her fingers running over his stomach, tracing maddening lines across his skin that had his need ramping up, until he was desperate to feel her against his hard length again.

As if she knew his need, she sat back on him.

She smiled wickedly and wriggled, tearing a groan from his throat as her warm heat enveloped his cock again. He had to be inside her now. He couldn't wait any longer.

He took hold of her hips and lifted her. His erection sprang up, hard and eager, and he shivered as she lowered her right hand and gripped it, positioning it beneath her. He moaned when she sank down onto his length, easing back onto it, drawing out the joining. An exquisite torture. He held his hips steady, resisting the temptation to thrust into her welcoming body.

When he was as deep as she could take him, she wriggled on him again, tearing another low groan from his throat, and then raised herself.

Apollyon grasped her hips, guiding her on his cock and helping her as she slowly sank back onto him and rose again. He thrust up into her as she came down, meeting her halfway, and steadily built the pace between them, until she was moaning with him each time their bodies met, his hard aching cock delving deep into her hot core.

He kept his eyes locked on her, watching the myriad of emotions that crossed her face as she rode him. She gasped when he plunged into her and moaned when he withdrew, her lips parted in ecstasy that flowed through him too.

She was divine and Edward was wrong about him.

He would never tire of her.

He would never leave her.

Because he was falling in love with her and he had been for a long time.

Her eyes met his and the world fell away.

He lost track of their movements until he was just looking into her eyes and feeling everything that she was, filled with the way it felt to be as one with her, inside her, together.

It awed him.

Her beauty and how it felt to be with her awed him. Not just like this either. He had made her happy and eased her suffering, but she had done the same for him too. He was happy again at last, content and no longer alone, and he knew that she would never leave him.

He could feel her love pounding through her veins and through him, could sense the affection she held for him and that she wanted this to go on forever too.

It was more than just being intimate with him, more than just lust.

It was about being one with him and sharing their love.

He loved her.

And she loved him.

Her heart beat with his, her hands pressing into his stomach as she moved on him, taking him deep into her body, joining them as one.

The stars behind her brightened, until they shone through the veil of light from the city and twinkled.

He sensed her power rising, calling to his own, entwining with it just as their bodies were.

The night became a beautiful backdrop for Serenity as she rode him, her eyes still locked with his. He released her hips, took hold of her hands and pressed his palms to hers as he linked their fingers, binding them in another way to each other.

The magic flowed into him, warming his fingers, and he let his power join with it.

A shooting star arced across the night sky above her, quickly followed by another.

She was making the night as beautiful as it should be—magical.

Apollyon stared deep into her hazel eyes. Under her spell. Forever and always.

Whether she knew it or not, she had cast a spell on him and he was powerless to break it. He didn't want to anyway. He wanted to be under her command when they were like this and just in life too. He wanted to be there to protect her, to make her smile, to give her happiness and everything that his angel deserved.

She writhed on him, taking him higher until he was in Heaven and flying with her.

Serenity leaned forwards, so her long blonde waves curled around her breasts, hiding them from his hungry eyes. Her hands left his and she planted them against his chest. He took hold of her hips, raised her almost all the way off his cock and plunged into her again, bringing her down harder now.

She cried out and dug her fingernails into his chest.

He did it again, and again, pushing her higher, until he felt her body tensing. He wanted to be one with her completely, wanted to fall into bliss with her and hold her close until they had both come down. He moved her again, bringing her down onto his cock, and she flung her head back and shouted his name, her body convulsing around his.

Apollyon didn't stop. He moved her on his cock, delving deeper into her, his body tightening with each long thrust, bringing him closer to the edge. He closed his eyes, groaning each time he buried himself in her and her body clenched him, quivering against him, luring him towards bliss. He wanted it. With a deep, growling groan, he quickened his pace until it bordered on frantic, searching for release, his whole body coiled tight and ready to explode.

"Apollyon," Serenity moaned and tensed her body around his, tipping him over the edge.

He plunged hard into her and shuddered as release blazed through him, his thrusts slowing until he was barely moving, his whole body shaking as hazy bliss ran in his veins.

Serenity collapsed onto him, breathing fast, her heart thundering against his, and he wrapped his arms around her and held her. A smile teased his lips when a blanket appeared and covered them. It wasn't his doing. It was his witch's.

He pressed a kiss to her forehead, savouring the feel of her in his arms and her body against his.

Bliss.

Serenity raised herself, her hands on his shoulders, and kissed him. He lazily returned the kiss, lost in her and thoughts of their future.

He would fly with her every night like this, would sleep with her tucked safely in his arms, and would watch over her so she was never alone. He would be with her forever, just as she had commanded him to be, and he would never let her go. He would do anything to make her smile, no matter how foolish it made him look or how silly her request.

For once in long millennia, he was happy and he wasn't alone.

His mission had changed the moment he had met her. He had changed and his allegiance was to her now, his new master. And what a divine creature she was.

Apollyon kissed her, slowing the tempo until they were drawing each one out, and held her close to him. He had waited for the call, for a new mission, for many long centuries and when it had finally come, it had given him more than just a task to fulfil.

It had given him Serenity.

His little witch.

His goddess.

And he would worship her forever.

**The End**

**Read on for a preview of the next book in the Her Angel: Bound Warriors Series, Fallen Angel!**

# FALLEN ANGEL

Lukas was looking worse for wear.

Annelie had never seen him drink alcohol. She had often wondered why he came to her pub but stuck to soft drinks. Seeing him slowly sliding down towards the wooden bar, his head propped up on his hand and his eyes closed, she was no longer surprised that he lay off the booze.

He couldn't handle it.

His scruffy sandy locks fell forwards when his head slipped from his hand and he jerked up.

He rolled his eyes a few times while blinking and then pulled a face as he inspected the damp elbow of his black shirt and the wet bar where he had been leaning.

A sigh lifted his broad shoulders and his green eyes shifted to the half-full glass of whisky in front of him, growing a little unfocused as he stared at it. He turned it on the bar, canting his head to his left as he studied it. The soft lighting above him reflected off the glass, casting patterns over the dark wood, and his gaze went from unfocused to hazy. Either he was lost in thought, or the whisky was really taking its toll on him.

Perhaps she should have cut him off after his third, but his charming smile had persuaded her to supply him with a fourth, and a fifth. She regretted it now, her stomach squirming whenever she looked at him and saw the effect of the alcohol on him.

At the time, he had looked as though he would be fine.

Now, he looked as though he was going to pass out.

Heck, maybe she shouldn't have given him the first shot.

What if he didn't drink because he was an alcoholic and she had just ruined his recovery?

She would never be able to live with herself if that was the case.

She handed some change to a patron and walked along the length of the area behind the bar to Lukas, neatening her appearance as she did so, a nervous habit she couldn't quite get under control whenever she was heading in his direction.

Her heart rate jacked up as she tugged the hem of her black baby-doll t-shirt down to sit smoothly along the waist of her black jeans and combed her fingers through her long red hair. She always felt as though she looked like a mess whenever things got frantic behind the bar.

And she wanted to look her best for Lukas.

She had been deeply aware of her appearance from the moment she had first set eyes on him, felt self-conscious whenever his eyes landed on her, and ached for them to return to her whenever he looked away.

Did he know how badly he affected her?

Did she affect him at all?

Her pulse raced faster and she struggled to breathe evenly as she neared him. They must have talked for hours in the years they had known each other, had shared secrets and laughs about all manner of things, but she still had to drag her courage up from her toes whenever she wanted to speak with him.

She nodded when an elderly man wished her a good night, offering him a warm smile that came straight from her heart. She had known him since she was a kid, back when her parents had run the old bar that was now hers and she had been more interested in running around and talking to all the regulars, showing them her latest paintings or hearing their stories.

Annelie glanced around to make sure that no one needed her.

The pub was quieter now that it was approaching closing time. A few regulars remained along with a group of people she didn't recognise who were sitting in the corner near the bay windows that overlooked the road.

She could finally speak to Lukas without interruption.

She sucked down a quiet breath.

Leaned on the damp bar opposite Lukas, between two sets of pumps.

Reached a trembling hand out and swept his fair hair out of his eyes.

He leaned away, almost fell off his stool, clutched the brass rail that ran around the edge of the bar to stop himself, and then looked at her.

An all-too-familiar jolt shot through her when his clear green eyes met her brown ones and her heart fluttered in her chest when he smiled lopsidedly.

"You okay?" She went to take her hand away but he took hold of it, bringing it down to the bar.

She swallowed hard as he toyed with her fingers, his warm and firm against them, and her heart thundered, hammering against her chest as her mouth dried out.

His gaze fell to their joined hands, a flicker of fascination entering his eyes, and she told herself not to read into it.

So what if this was the first bordering-on-intimate contact they'd had?

So what if he had made her heart stop the moment he had first walked into her pub three years ago and it had stopped every time she had seen him since?

It didn't mean anything.

At least, it didn't mean anything to him.

Sure, they had talked and whiled away the hours, and Lukas was an amazing listener and always seemed genuinely interested in her problems and helping her solve them, but he had never once shown any interest in her beyond friendship.

She wished that he would.

He was drop dead gorgeous. Six feet plus of masculine beauty. And she wanted to pounce on him whenever he walked through the door.

Which had been almost every other night until recently.

He had gone away for three long weeks without a word, leaving her wondering if something terrible had happened to him.

And then the moment he walked back into her life, he hit the drink.

Hard.

Lukas didn't answer her. His green gaze remained fixed on her hand and he turned it this way and that, his touch gentle now. Her heart whispered that this was interest beyond friendship. She tried to shut it up but it persisted, filled her head with the ridiculous thought that she might finally get her wish, that those dreams she had of Lukas were finally going to become real.

Annelie shut it down, because disappointment and heartache lay down that road.

Lukas was just drunk, tired and, by the looks of things, a little out of sorts. For the first time, he looked as if he was the one who needed to unburden his shoulders and his heart, and she was determined to listen to him as he had listened to her so many times in the past. She was going to help him. It was the least she could do for him.

Someone stepped up to the bar at the far end and she waved to Andy to serve him. She couldn't leave Lukas until she knew what was going on in his head and why he was suddenly drinking, or at least until she was sure he wasn't about to fall off his stool and hurt himself.

Annelie bent lower so she could see his face.

His gaze finally left her hand and met hers again, bright in the lights from the mirrored cabinet of bottles behind her.

"I said you okay?" She searched his eyes.

His pupils were wide as he raked his gaze down over her chest, fire following in its wake, and then lifted it back up to her face. It remained fixed there and a blush crept onto her cheeks as he studied her, the intensity and sudden sharpness of his eyes holding her captive even when she wanted to glance away and avoid his gaze. He had never looked at her so closely, or with so much banked heat in his eyes.

Heat that rippled through her and had her deeply aware of the way his hand held hers and how close she was to him.

"Hell of a week." His reply was so quiet that she barely heard him.

"You've been gone three." Those words slipped from her lips before she could stop them, laced with hurt that surprised her, had her reeling a little as she stared at him and felt the heavy press of that pain on her heart.

She had thought she had been worried about Lukas when he had disappeared on her, but now she realised it had hurt her too. She had been afraid she would never see him again.

His eyebrows rose. "Three?"

Annelie nodded. Lukas released her hand and she mourned the loss of contact, ached for him to touch her again, to hold her because it had been reassuring her that he was back with her now.

He heaved a long sigh and ran his hand over the messy finger-length strands of his hair, preening it back, before pinching the bridge of his nose. His eyes screwed shut.

"Hell of a three weeks." Lukas smiled but she saw straight through it.

Something was wrong.

"Annelie," Andy called but she waved him away again.

Andy had been tending bar long enough to handle problems on his own now.

Lukas needed to talk. She had seen it the moment he had sat down tonight, but the pub had been so busy that she hadn't been able to talk to him other than taking his order. He had never really spoken much about himself and the one time he needed to, she hadn't made time for him.

He had always made time to listen to her.

What sort of friend was she?

"I was wondering where you were." Her tone was jest but her heart meant the words, ached a little as the last three weeks caught up with her together with the revelation that she had been afraid of never seeing him again.

Lukas's eyes lifted back to meet hers, and she told herself not to read into the look that crossed his handsome face, because there was a chance she was misinterpreting it or just seeing what she wanted to see—that he was pleased to hear she had missed him, had been thinking about him.

He dropped his green gaze back to his whisky glass and ran a finger around the rim of it. "Sorry about that."

She never had been able to place his accent.

It wasn't British like hers and most of the people who frequented the pub.

She had asked him about it once and he had simply said that he had lived in many places. She had told him her whole life story and he hadn't even told her where he was from. If she asked again, would he tell her? If she didn't give up this time and tried to peel back his layers to learn more about him, would he answer all her questions?

She had never pressed him before, had secretly enjoyed the air of mystery that surrounded him, but now things were different. He had gone away, and had returned a different man, and she wanted to know where he had been, what he had done, and why he had disappeared. She wanted to know everything about him.

He picked up his glass and she took it from him.

"I think you've had enough of that." She tipped the contents in the sink behind the bar and stashed the glass there. "How are you getting home tonight?"

He frowned, propped his head up on his palm, and closed his eyes. "The usual way."

She shook her head at that. "I can't let you drive."

A smile curved his profane lips. "I don't drive. I fly."

"Well, I can't let you drink and fly." She couldn't contain the laugh that bubbled up, shook her head for a different reason as she looked at him.

He was drunk if he thought he could fly home.

Annelie covered his other hand with hers and he opened his eyes, their green depths meeting hers again. They were sharper now but not enough to satisfy her.

"I'll give you a lift if you wait until we've closed." Hopefully he would have sobered up a little by then and could direct her to his place.

She had never seen him outside work before and didn't have a clue about where he lived. She thought she remembered him mentioning it was in the city, somewhere close to the heart of London, but she couldn't be sure.

Lukas stared into her eyes for what felt like hours and then nodded.

Annelie took her hand back and smiled, relief flowing through her. It was better he didn't go home alone, in a cab or on the bus. She would only end up worrying that he had gotten into trouble somewhere.

Or might disappear again.

While she was driving him, she was going to get him to talk to her. She was going to find out where he had gone and why he was suddenly drinking. She was going to ease the weight on his shoulders just as he had done for her so many times in the past.

Closing time was only twenty minutes away, but it would be at least another hour before she had finished cleaning up, counting the takings and getting everything ready for tomorrow.

She glanced back at Lukas and debated making him a coffee to help him sober up.

He rested his arm on the counter and used it as a pillow, his eyes closing again. Sleep would probably help him as much as caffeine. He had looked tired before he had started drinking, worn down and in need of a good night's rest.

She turned towards the rows of bottles and optics and turned off the sound system, so only the chatter of the other patrons filled the pub. Hopefully the hum of voices wouldn't disturb Lukas.

Annelie flinched when Andy called for last orders, his voice loud enough to wake the neighbourhood, and scowled at him. He gave her a blank look. She jerked her chin towards Lukas where he was sleeping, and Andy's dark eyebrows lifted as his gaze shifted to him and then a mischievous smile lit his face as he looked back at her.

"He sleeping over?" Andy parked his hip against the bar near her as she served a customer.

"I'm taking him home." She shot Andy a look when he grinned at her. "It's not like that. I'm just going to drive him home and drop him off."

He didn't look as if he believed her.

"Just serve the customers." She shoved him playfully in his chest and he winked and went to work.

Her gaze crept back to Lukas, heart fluttering in her throat as she thought about driving him home and the way he had held her hand, had played with her fingers and had looked at her with a wicked edge to his eyes, a flare of desire that echoed inside her.

Did he want her, or was it just the booze talking?

She barely noticed the pub emptying, was too swept up in her thoughts to say goodbye to everyone as she got a head start on cleaning up.

"I'm out." Andy tossed his towel down at the other end of the bar. "You be good now."

Annelie ignored that. "Night."

He moved out from behind the bar, grabbed his coat and stopped behind Lukas.

She scowled at Andy when he clutched his hands together in front of his chest, twisted back and forth at the waist and fluttered his eyelashes as if he was swooning over Lukas.

"Get out of here before I fire your arse." She lifted her own towel, scrunched it up in her hand and threatened to throw it at him.

He grinned, turned on his heel and strode towards the door. "Don't do anything I wouldn't."

She shook her head. There wasn't much Andy wouldn't do.

The door closed and she shifted her focus to Lukas where he leaned over the bar, sound asleep. Her pulse thrummed, steadily picking up pace as she gazed at him and grew aware of the fact she was alone with him now.

Damn, he was gorgeous even when he was drunk, drew her to him like no other man had before him.

She shook herself out of her reverie, tied her long red hair back into a ponytail and wiped the bar down, doing her best not to disturb Lukas and trying to avoid looking at him.

It didn't work.

She found herself stood by him, looking down at his face, watching him sleep. A need poured through her, swirled and gained strength, until she couldn't resist it. She hesitated and then, with her heart in her mouth, brushed the tangled strands of his fair hair from his forehead.

His firm lips parted and he murmured something.

She smiled and brushed his skin again, lightly so he wouldn't wake, but enough contact to make her feel a little giddy.

When had she fallen for him?

It had come on so slowly over the past three years that she hadn't realised she had those sorts of feelings for Lukas until he had gone away, and then she had been worried that he wasn't coming back.

But here he was again, at her bar in the same stool he always occupied, bringing light into her life and her heart in that way only he could, making the days without him disappear.

A smile tugged at her lips. She had never been happier to see him.

Even if he was asleep.

He stirred and blinked slowly, as though trying to wake himself.

Annelie didn't take her hand back. She was feeling brave tonight, a little courageous and bold, willing to take a risk and see what happened.

"How are you feeling?" She combed her fingers through his hair.

Lukas frowned, his green eyes fixed on the distance, and then groaned. She took that as a negative answer.

"No better yet?" Her gaze followed her fingers as she stroked them down the curve of his left ear.

He nodded, moving her hand with him, and a smile touched his lips and then faded again when he closed his eyes.

"I'm almost done. I'll have you home soon." She went to walk away.

He caught her wrist so fast that it startled her, his grip firm as he sat up, and looked at her with such earnest eyes that her heart beat harder and a rush of nerves surged through her.

"I ever tell you that you're pretty?" Those words, spoken in a low husky voice, rocked her to her core.

Her pulse raced and her throat turned dry. She shook her head and he reached out with his other hand and ran the backs of his fingers down her cheek, his caress light but setting her nerve-endings aflame and sending a hot shiver over her skin. Her lips parted as she searched his eyes, trying to see if he knew what he was saying, and whether he believed she was pretty.

There was nothing but honesty and warmth in them.

They sparkled with it, looking brighter now even though the lights were lower, entrancing her. "Your beauty puts angels to shame."

Annelie tried to convince herself that it was the drink talking but failed dismally.

She had worked in the pub since she was in her early twenties, almost ten years ago, and had run it since her parents had retired early. She had enough experience to spot levels of inebriation.

Lukas's eyes were sharper and his words weren't slurred. He wasn't drunk anymore.

He was definitely still tipsy, but that excuse didn't hold with her heart.

It believed him.

He really did think that she was beautiful.

She blushed. It burned her cheeks before she could get the better of herself. She worked at a bar. She was used to men telling her that she was beautiful at the end of the night, but the way Lukas said it, the fact that it was him, made her believe him.

"You really are." His hand slipped from her cheek to her jaw and he grazed his fingers along the curve of it. He smiled and her heart thudded. *He* was beautiful. She had never seen a man like him, with such deep green eyes and a smile that could make her heart pound and body tremble. "Beautiful."

"Hush." She took his hand away from her face and held it a moment. "Quit making me blush, Lukas."

His smile held. "I love the way you say my name. Say it again."

Annelie rolled her eyes. "Lukas."

"Not like that." He drew his hand towards him, luring her with it, until she was close to him. She stared down into his eyes, her mind racing forwards to contemplate things it shouldn't be. He wasn't going to kiss her. Even if he was looking more sober now, she couldn't let things go down that avenue. His eyes fell to her lips and then lifted to meet hers again. "Say it like you mean it. Like you said it just then."

Annelie looked deep into his eyes, lost in them and the way the flecks of pale gold seemed to shift and move against their emerald backdrop, and blinked slowly.

Her voice dropped to a whisper. "Lukas."

"Mmm, that's more like it." He pulled her closer and tilted his head.

Her gaze dropped to his mouth, heart hammering against her ribs and blood thundering as a need to kiss him bolted through her, lighting her up inside, making her sway towards him.

Just one kiss.

## FALLEN ANGEL

Cast out of Heaven for a crime he didn't commit, Lukas has spent three years searching for a way to prove his innocence and slowly falling for a beautiful mortal female. When things take a turn for the worse, he seeks solace in the bottom of a bottle and ends up finding it in Annelie's arms. But one moment of Heaven becomes one of sheer Hell when his wings make an unexpected appearance. Now, he's in danger of losing not only his duty, but the woman he loves.

Annelie fell for Lukas the moment he walked into her bar and she fell hard. The tall, sensual blond sets her heart on fire with his otherworldly green eyes and wicked smile, so when one kiss leads to something more, seizing her chance and Lukas with both hands seems like a great idea… until morning rolls around and she discovers he's not the man she thought he was—he's an angel.

Lukas will stop at nothing to prove both his innocence and his love for Annelie, but when he discovers who framed him and she ends up caught in the crossfire, will he be strong enough to protect her? And can Annelie vanquish her doubts and fears to claim the heart of her fallen angel?

**Available November 30th 2018 in ebook and paperback**

# ABOUT THE AUTHOR

Felicity Heaton is a New York Times and USA Today best-selling author who writes passionate paranormal romance books. In her books she creates detailed worlds, twisting plots, mind-blowing action, intense emotion and heart-stopping romances with leading men that vary from dark deadly vampires to sexy shape-shifters and wicked werewolves, to sinful angels and hot demons!

If you're a fan of paranormal romance authors Lara Adrian, J R Ward, Sherrilyn Kenyon, Gena Showalter, Larissa Ione and Christine Feehan then you will enjoy her books too.

If you love your angels a little dark and wicked, her best-selling Her Angel romance series is for you. If you like strong, powerful, and dark vampires then try the Vampires Realm romance series or any of her stand alone vampire romance books. If you're looking for vampire romances that are sinful, passionate and erotic then try her Vampire Erotic Theatre romance series. Or if you like hot-blooded alpha heroes who will let nothing stand in the way of them claiming their destined woman then try her Eternal Mates series. It's packed with sexy heroes in a world populated by elves, vampires, fae, demons, shifters, and more. If sexy Greek gods with incredible powers battling to save our world and their home in the Underworld are more your thing, then be sure to step into the world of Guardians of Hades.

If you have enjoyed this story, please take a moment to contact the author at **author@felicityheaton.com** or to post a review of the book online

**Connect with Felicity:**
Website – http://www.felicityheaton.com
Blog – http://www.felicityheaton.com/blog/
Twitter – http://twitter.com/felicityheaton
Facebook – http://www.facebook.com/felicityheaton
Goodreads – http://www.goodreads.com/felicityheaton
Mailing List – http://www.felicityheaton.com/newsletter.php

**FIND OUT MORE ABOUT HER BOOKS AT:**
**http://www.felicityheaton.com**